MW00912218

Making the Cut

Revolution Hockey Series

Bradley J Burton

Tellwell Talent
www.tellwell.ca

ISBN
978-0-2288-3265-2 (Paperback)
978-0-2288-3266-9 (eBook)

A CHAMPIONSHIP IN THE MAKING

"We're one period away from accomplishing our goal, boys!" DJ Roberts stood confidently in front of his teammates in the locker room. "We have some work to do to get back into this one, but I believe in each and every one of you in this room! This is a brotherhood in here—a bond like nothing else I have experienced. We ride together, and we die together! But, boys... we aren't dying tonight! Let's go win a championship!"

The room roared in approval of their captain's motivating speech and they charged out of the dressing room. The Steelers AAA Minor Midget tcam was ready to attempt a comeback from a 3–1 deficit in the final period of the Ontario Championships against the Flying Jets.

The skaters made their way to the opening faceoff for the third period. Brad Martinsen squared off with his adversary and the two centres battled for possession as the ref dropped the puck. Marty was able to work the puck free and had help from DJ to win the puck back to their defenceman. Victor Sharp took control of the puck and skated up the wall before being forced to chip it high into the offensive zone.

Mike McDennis flanked DJ and Marty on their right side and tracked down the dumped puck. The Flying Jets' defender scooped up possession and knew he was under pressure. McDennis raced after him as the puck carrier circled behind the net and up the left wall. DJ and Marty did their best to isolate time and space away from their opponent, but a quick cross-ice flip pushed the Steelers back onto the defensive side of the ice. Sharp backtracked and watched as the puck floated through the air, however, he was unable to take the risk of retrieving it as two Flying Jet forwards pursued the clearance as well.

The Flying Jets garnered up possession and charged down on Sharp and his defensive partner, Dave Gillies. It was a 3-on-2 attack, although DJ and Marty were hot on the heels of the streaking forwards. Sharp and Gillies defended the rush well and allowed their backchecking forwards an opportunity to help defensively. Marty put immediate back pressure on the puck carrier and forced him to try a drop pass to the high guy in the slot. However, DJ's coverage was precise and he swept his stick to break up the play swiftly.

The puck deflected to the boards and DJ broke away from his defensive assignment and quickly gathered it up. He took a quick glance up the ice and saw McDennis darting through the middle of the ice, poised for a pass. DJ instinctively ripped it out to his teammate and dug in to join him on the rush.

McDennis cradled the puck and skated hard down toward the opposing net. He shielded the puck from the defender as he gained a slight edge in position on the defenceman. The defender played him strong and prevented him from a direct path to the net, so McDennis slammed on the breaks—shooting snow high into the air. The move surprised the defender and he created some room for himself.

"Mikey!" shouted DJ as he filtered into the offensive zone.

McDennis heard DJ call for the puck and delivered a quick pass to his captain in the high slot. DJ walked right into the perfectly placed pass and wasted no time teeing off a one-timer on net. The puck rocketed off his stick and beat the outstretched glove of the goaltender—bringing the Steelers to within one goal on the scoreboard. DJ raised his arms in celebration and was quickly mobbed by his teammates on the ice.

"Great shot, DJ!" said Marty. "Awesome play, Mikey!"

"Let's keep it going!" said DJ as he darted toward the Steelers' bench to celebrate.

The Steelers dug in deep and simplified their game to apply more pressure on the Flying Jets' defence. Line after line and shift after shift, the Steelers got the puck in behind their opponents and crashed and banged in the corner. Cam Zalapski and Chase Livermore were seeing the best results from the new strategy.

Livermore was displaying his excellent two-way game and worked relentlessly on the backcheck to create turnovers; he demonstrated this in fine fashion as the clock ticked under the five-minute mark. Livermore guided the oncoming skater toward the boards and used a well-timed stick check to create a turnover in the neutral zone. He immediately took control of the puck and saw an oncoming defender tracking him from the middle. Without hesitation Livermore dumped the puck deep.

The Flying Jets' goaltender came out to play the puck, as he looked to help his defenceman who were being worn out by the dump-and-chase game. Zalapski hustled in on the weak side and worked in the goaltender's blind spot—surprising the goaltender in behind the net.

"Rim it! Rim it!" cried out the Flying Jets' defenceman as he witnessed Zalapski closing in. However, it was too late and the puck was stripped away. Zalapski took a look out into the slot and saw Victor Sharp busting in toward the empty net. With a hard snap of the stick, Zalapski passed the puck out for the tap-in tying goal. The Steelers' bench erupted with joy and the players on the ice swarmed together to celebrate. As the players went by with their celebratory high-fives, the line of Marty, DJ and McDennis hopped out onto the ice and prepared for the upcoming draw.

"Here we go, Sammy!" said DJ as he circled back to his goaltender, Sam Nectle. He tapped Nectle on the pad before racing up to his position for the faceoff. DJ had been working hard the whole game. He was a key component in the Flying Jets' defensive game plan—which meant he received much physical attention throughout the game. However, the tying goal sent a surge of energy throughout his body and he felt electrified.

The puck dropped to the ice once again, with the Flying Jets pouncing on the puck first. They wasted no time directing it down into the offensive zone. It shot directly in on Nectle and with the opposition roaring in on his defence, he decided to hold on for a whistle. Marty squared up for the defensive zone faceoff, but he was tied up off the draw. The Flying Jets seemed intent on recapturing their vanquished lead, and they had caught the Steelers off guard—gaining control of the puck. With the Steelers playing on their heels, the Flying Jets wheeled around the offensive zone and opened up with a few quick shots—all turned away effectively by Nectle.

"Settle down out there, boys," the Steelers' coach hollered.

The five players on the ice quit chasing the game and moved into a passive and composed defensive formation. They allowed the Flying Jets to work the puck on the perimeter but prevented them from accessing any dangerous scoring areas.

Victor Sharp guarded his corner effectively, and executed a brilliant stick check to knock the puck off the stick of the pressing forward. A loose puck battle commenced in the corner to the left of Nectle. Sharp fought hard with his opponent, but a secondary forward swooped in and carried the puck behind the net. Marty tracked the skater and pressed hard, stripping his opponent of possession.

DJ was playing in the slot as he watched his centre perform the defensive maneuver and he quickly remembered the brief talk they had ahead of the period. He jolted into action and streaked out of the defensive zone. Marty took one quick look and masterfully executed a hard stretch pass that sailed out into the neutral zone and onto DJ's stick as he broke in behind the defence.

DJ charged down the ice on a breakaway and was clean in from centre. He watched as the goaltender challenged him far outside the crease—DJ knew his speed on the approach could really cause problems for the goalie's aggressive tactic. The goalie backtracked slowly and methodically as DJ closed in. DJ moved into the slot and pulled the puck quickly onto his forehand—releasing a low, fast shot. The goalie was late to react and the puck whistled through his legs and into the back of the net. DJ raised his arms and curled off into the corner before being charged by his linemates.

"Oh my goodness, DJ!" Marty yelled. "That was unbelievable!"

"Straight out of the playbook, baby!" said DJ. As they raced back toward their bench, DJ glanced up at the scoreboard. It now read 4–3 for the Steelers and there was only 3:06 remaining in the third period.

Knowing the battle was far from over, DJ remained focused and eager to defend their first lead of the game. Out on the ice, the tandem of Zalapski and Livermore provided some top-notch checking as they prevented the Flying Jets from escaping their half of the ice over the course of their 46-second shift, bringing the clock down to 2:20 remaining. The Steelers' top line returned to the ice for the upcoming offensive zone draw.

Marty aligned his wingers up for the draw—stacking the middle of the ice. Using a quick stick, Marty scooped the puck as it fell to the ice and in one motion directed it back toward DJ. It was a bit off, but DJ extended his stick and cradled the puck inward. He knew he would have to release it promptly as the defenders closed his space rapidly. The shot flew off his stick toward the goal and cleared all the traffic on the way through, but the Flying Jets' goaltender kicked out his left pad and directed it out to the boards.

The Flying Jets' pounced on the loose puck and transitioned up the ice quickly. Knowing they needed to push for the tying goal, all five skaters pressed up on the attack. The goaltender looked to the bench and received the signal to vacate the ice to allow an extra attacker to join the play. The Flying Jets' drove the puck into the Steelers' zone and put an all-out attack on the defenders. They regained control of the puck and proceeded to look for their next mark with a 6-on-5 advantage.

"Empty net!" shrieked the players on the Steelers' bench as they tried to inform their teammates.

It only seemed to be a matter of time before the Flying Jets would attempt a play at the net. They worked a 2-on-1 on Dave Gillies and were finally able to break down the coverage as the defenceman tried to break up the passing sequence, but missed the puck. This allowed the Flying Jets a quick opportunity to force the net with possession out of the corner. Marty was forced to leap into action as he dropped down to prevent a clean lane to the net—this in turn opened up the shooter in the slot. The pass eluded Marty, and DJ and McDennis were just a stick length away from the sniper, but were unable to stop him from connecting on a one-timer. The shot sizzled off the blade of the stick and was destined to find the back of the cage. Sam Nectle tracked the play soundly and as the puck moved toward the shooter, he pushed out to cut down the angle as much as possible. He watched as the shot rocketed off the stick and came barrelling in on him—leaving him with a split second to react.

THUD!

Nectle's outstretched glove connected with the goal-bound puck as he snagged it in dramatic fashion. The Steelers' bench went wild at the sight of the fabulous stop.

TWEET...

The whistle sounded to bring the game to a stoppage in play.

"Unreal save, Sammy!" DJ said, as he patted his goalie on the helmet.

"Thanks, DJ," said the calm and cool goaltender. "Just doing my part!"

DJ looked to his bench to see whether there would be a line change, but could see that his coach was signalling for a time out instead. DJ nodded to his coach and quickly motioned to the referee that the Steelers would like to use up their team time out.

The ref blew his whistle. "Time out, Steelers!" he announced to the scorekeeper.

The players from both teams returned to their respective benches for instruction. The break in play came with 1:18 left on the clock.

"We need to remain strong in front of the net and take away the middle of the ice," explained the Steelers' coach. "This is a big draw, Marty. We need it!"

TWEET...

The whistle from the ref announced the end of the allotted 30 seconds for the timeout.

The players broke from the huddle at the bench and Marty geared up for the draw once again, but he was overly eager and swung prior to the linesman dropping the puck. The linesman stood upright from his crouched position and motioned Marty out of the faceoff circle. McDennis swapped positions with him, but lost cleanly to the Flying Jets' top faceoff man.

The defenceman took control of the puck and skated across the top of the offensive zone and fired a quick shot toward the net. The puck cleared everyone in the slot, but it was wide of the net and bounced off the end wall where Gillies was able to whack it hard around the boards. DJ skated hard to the wall where he anticipated the puck would be and was engaged by a pinching defenceman. The two clashed as they battled for the puck on the boards. DJ chipped the puck behind his opponent and out toward the blueline, but the Flying Jets' support fired the puck back into the corner.

Gillies was first to the puck and tried to clear the zone immediately, however he had two oncoming players converge on him and knock down the lob shot. The Flying Jets gained full control of the puck in the corner and were more aggressive on this possession than the prior one. The forwards worked the puck down low and across to the weak side of the ice—where their extra-man waited patiently.

"Protect the net!" pleaded the Steelers' bench.

The Flying Jets' attacker met the puck in stride as it came to him on the right side of Nectle. Without hesitation, he stepped out from behind the goal line and jammed the puck—trying to forcefully push the puck over the line for a goal.

The Steelers dropped down to help out with the net battle. Bodies started dropping as players desperately fought on both sides of the play. The puck remained in the scrum until it was finally pulled out by an attacking player.

The clock was now under 30 seconds as the Flying Jets moved the puck to their defenceman. DJ raced out to the point and looked to stay in the shooting lane. With the path to the net excellently closed off, the defenceman pivoted and skated the puck down the boards as he tried to protect the puck from his checker.

DJ was persistent and determined to create a turnover. Staying with his man, DJ aggressively reached in for a poke check. He knocked the puck off his opponent's stick and into the corner. The two continued down to the loose puck and engaged physically as they closed in on it. DJ got the better of his opponent and knocked him off balance—allowing a split second to try a clearing attempt. With a quick flick, DJ lofted the puck high into the sky—it barely cleared the rafters and landed in the neutral zone.

3… 2… 1… BUZZ!

The Steelers charged off the bench with gloves and sticks flying in every direction. They barrelled in and stormed Sam

Nectle off his feet. DJ was exhausted from his on-ice battle, but exerted his last bit of energy to join the pile up in the crease.

DJ broke free to find his linemate and best friend. "We did it, Marty!" he shouted as the two embraced each other in a celebratory hug.

"This moment is surreal," said Marty. "What a way to end the year—champions!"

"Whoo!" responded DJ. "Oh yeah! We are the champions…"

CHAPTER I

THE EARLY RISER

BEEP... BEEP... BEEP...

The alarm burst to life at the early hour of 5:00 am. Suddenly, the owner reached across the side table and picked up his cell phone. With a quick touch and flip of the screen, the sound vanished. Still laying on his back, DJ Roberts closed his eyes as he visualized the upcoming day.

The day consisted of what many others in the previous three to four months had: hard work. Unlike the other days which were filled with morning and afternoon training sessions, this one was the one that all that hard work went into fulfilling. This morning, he would march down to his hometown arena and lace up his skates to try out for the new Junior A hockey team: the Revolution.

DJ had been looking forward to this day since the announcement of the team's creation—which happened almost immediately after his AAA Minor Midget season had ended. After being drafted to Sarnia of the Major Junior league in the spring, DJ made his decision to try to obtain a scholarship from a school in the United States. He turned down the offer to join the Major Junior team knowing that it would disqualify him from achieving his goal. This choice left DJ open to pretty well any team of his choosing when it came to gearing up for the upcoming year—and his hometown team became the primary target. Influencing DJ's choice to pursue a spot with the Revolution, was their appointed General Manager, Bob Flaherty. GM Flaherty and DJ had already developed a strong relationship, as the GM was his mathematics teacher and hockey coach at the high school. GM Flaherty had a thorough love for the game of hockey and the two would frequently engage in "hockey talk." DJ knew he could confide in GM Flaherty and would often look to him for mentorship, as well. The two regularly discussed DJ's future and goals—and he was a huge advocate for DJ to pursue a scholarship. GM Flaherty made it very clear that DJ would be well represented and able to showcase himself at a very competitive level if he were to make the Revolution.

Additionally, DJ's best friend had many discussions with him regarding the upcoming hockey season. Brad Martinsen, or Marty for short, was not only his friend, but had been his centre for the majority of their last six years playing AAA hockey together. Marty was a very creative and agile middleman, and with DJ's speed and scoring touch on the wing, the two created a potent 1-2 punch. Marty was in a similar situation, as both players had impressed the scouts with their play and were very sought-after in the spring priority draft. However, the two players had similar ideas for their futures and were in full support of one another as they worked together to achieve success. With this as their pilot for the off-season, the two worked harder than ever to ensure they were in peak physical condition entering training camp—they worked out twice a day. The workouts consisted of muscular and endurance training, as well as on-ice training to develop and enhance their skills.

While these thoughts ran through DJ's mind as he kept warm under his covers, he immediately broke his concentration and sprang to his feet. DJ had reached a new level of excitement and anticipation. For many years he had engaged in a battle for supremacy amongst his own age category, but today he would be up against players anywhere from being the same age to players that were 20 years old. The difference would increase the challenge, but junior hockey would provide a new stage for him to elevate his game, and he was undeniably eager over the opportunity in front of him. As a 16-year-old, DJ was vying for one of two underage positions on the team, but ultimately he was looking for more than just that. He was battling it out for a prominent place at the top of the forward crew that would lead the Revolution franchise in season one.

He threw on his sweats and raced down the stairs to the kitchen. He was greeted by his parents, who were already up and eagerly ready to take on the day. "Morning, DJ," said his dad as he sat at the kitchen counter with a coffee in hand and the newspaper spread before him.

"Morning, Dad!"

"Good morning, son," his mom said as she came over to give him a hug. "We hope you have a great skate this morning. Breakfast is ready for you on the counter."

"Morning, Mom. Thanks!" DJ walked over to pick up his plate and then joined his parents at the table.

"Pretty excited, I'm assuming?" asked his father.

"Oh yeah! Marty and I have been working hard all summer long—this couldn't have come quick enough for us."

"Speaking of Marty, do you guys know if you are on the same squad yet?" his mom asked.

"Not to start, but hopefully they reunite us at some point," DJ answered.

The start of the training camp saw all the players split into two squads—Navy and Silver. DJ landed on the Navy squad, while Marty ended up on the Silver squad. This meant the two running mates would have to face each other in the intersquad games that would happen over the course of the camp. The first matchup was today at 3:00 pm.

"To be honest," his father said, "they probably want to see how you guys will do without each other. You guys obviously know each other inside and out, but…" he said with a bit of a pause, "you guys are competing for a spot on the team."

"Yeah, we know…"

"I mean," his father continued, "if they can only take two underage players, it is best if they see you as individuals. I heard the Anderson twins were trying out with the team too, and they both have a legitimate chance of making the team as well."

"Right." DJ knew his dad was making a valid point. The Andersons had been rivals of DJ and Marty's AAA hockey team for the past few seasons. They were admiral opponents and were quite capable of making the leap to play Junior A hockey.

"And you know there are more underagers on the ice too. I just don't want you to think that because of your connection with Mr. Flaherty you have an automatic spot on this team. That is not how things happen… at least not how they should. You need to show you belong, and that means that you need to be at your very best."

"I'm ready, Dad! But… I get your point." DJ was not demoralized by his dad's comments, as he very clearly understood that he needed to make a case for himself on the ice. His ultimate goal for the upcoming season was to be a leader on the team and he knew it would take continuous effort in order to be that type of player with the Revolution.

"Anyway," his mother interjected, "what's the game plan for today? Are we all going down to the arena together or…?"

"Well, I thought I could drop DJ off then swing back home and we could make our way down for when he hits the ice at 10:00 am. If that works for you, dear?"

"Yes, that should be fine," Mrs. Roberts responded to her husband.

"Perfect. Well, DJ… do what you need to do and let me know when you're ready to head out."

"Will do!" DJ finished up eating his breakfast and began to get everything else in order to take on the day.

CHAPTER II

THE REVOLUTION STAFF

The morning began with the same kind of dash and anticipation in the homes of many other members of the training camp, but none quite the same as newly-named Head Coach Steve Fitzgerald. Coach Fitzgerald woke up bright and early at a local bed and breakfast—he was still in the process of transitioning back home. The last five seasons of his life had been spent in Germany, playing professional hockey as he closed in on the end of his playing career. This year, he would transition from being on the ice to his new home supporting the Revolution players on the bench.

Coach Fitzgerald vacated his room around 6:00 am and set off to meet with his colleagues at the Memorial Arena. After making a quick stop at The Coffee Shop, he made his way down to the arena to meet with the rest of the Revolution staff—GM Bob Flaherty, Assistant GM Doug Chambers and Assistant Coaches Larry McIntosh and Craig Horton.

The Revolution staff had a few items to address on their agenda and at the forefront of the conversation was the topic of their underage situation. Heading into their training camp, the team knew they had amassed a young core of players—many who would be vying for two available positions. This group included talents such as DJ Roberts, Brad Martinsen, Nolan Anderson, Nathan Anderson, Eric Matheson and Victor Sharp. Matheson and Sharp were both budding defensive talents and very much part of the staff's conversation heading into the camp.

Eric Matheson, who played with the Anderson twins growing up, was a very good two-way defender and displayed tremendous skating ability. Much like Matheson, Victor Sharp played in all situations and excelled at skating. Alongside DJ and Marty, Sharp helped lead his team to a AAA Minor Midget championship the previous season. Both defencemen were extremely important contributors to their respective teams' success and were both viewed highly by the Revolution staff.

After the initial greetings took place, GM Flaherty dove right into the agenda. "Okay, fellas, today we finally get a chance to see the pieces fall into place. All the time and commitment that was put into making today successful will hopefully feel worthwhile."

"Agreed," said the other members of the staff in unison.

"So, here is where we stand heading into this morning," Flaherty continued. "We have four forwards signed, two defencemen and one goalie. That means we are in search of at least eight forwards, four defencemen and one more goaltender over the course of this training camp. We have the ability to sign up to 25 cards, two of which will be underage players. Having said that, the two underage players—and we have plenty of talent to choose from—must be key contributors to the team."

Coach Fitzgerald saw this pause as an opportunity to add to Flaherty's statement. "And the two underage players, from what we have discussed, will have every opportunity to prove themselves in my lineup. From the onset, I was open about wanting to build this franchise through youth, and I am very willing to use my young players in key roles."

"Exactly," responded GM Flaherty. "That is our goal. And that is—in my opinion—a way to achieve some form of success in this league in our inaugural season. The top teams in this league possess many talented 19- and 20-year-old hockey players, and we can't change that. The skill and experience that those players possess is tough to match. However, the insertion of youth and exuberance to our lineup could provide us with a strong foundation to build on going forward."

"Mix that with the few veteran players we have been able to acquire leading into camp," Assistant GM Chambers added, "and I think we will be able to ice a competitive team from the onset of this organization."

"On that note, let's go through the players we have already brought in and what our expectations of them are," said GM Flaherty. "Want to give us the rundown, Doug?"

"Would be my pleasure, Bob," responded Assistant GM Doug Chambers. He flipped open his binder, bringing up some player profiles he had put together.

"Before you get started, Doug," interrupted Coach Fitzgerald, "what is the word on Kip Kelley?"

"Glad you asked," said GM Flaherty. "He, as of last night, is officially the newest member of the Revolution."

"Wow! Great news!" replied Coach Fitzgerald.

"Yes, indeed," added Assistant GM Chambers. "Kelley is returning after spending the last two years playing Major Junior hockey in Ottawa. He wasn't quite getting what he was wanting up there and when he heard that our new team would be coming to town, he jumped on the idea of becoming the hometown hero once again. He attended camp up in Ottawa over the previous weekend and finally came to terms with them—parting ways this past week."

"And has guaranteed to sign a card before hitting the ice this morning!" GM Flaherty added with a smile. "His two-way game, scoring touch and experience will be crucial to our early success as an organization—and he will be an important cog in the development of young players, too."

"Exactly," replied Assistant GM Chambers. "Continuing on, we have added JJ Turcotte, James Northgate and Harrison Gage to the core up front."

Assistant Coach McIntosh piped up, "Turcotte has the offensive prowess to lead a second line. I've coached him a few times over the last several seasons and he may have the most pure offensive talent I've ever had an opportunity to work with."

"Yes, we are well aware of his offensive upside," responded GM Flaherty. "Let's just hope that his motivation is there to help him develop into a more complete player."

The rest of the staff nodded in agreement to both statements.

"Tell me about Northgate and Gage?" said Coach Fitzgerald.

"James Northgate is a big, nasty right wing," Assistant GM Chambers stated. "He didn't play much in Owen Sound over the last two seasons, but he gained a reputation in the Major Junior league as a player not to mess with. With a bunch of young bucks likely to debut in junior hockey this season, I can't think of a more valuable pickup than Northgate. He will ensure that our players are well taken care of!"

"Yes, I can't understate the value of a player like that," agreed Coach Fitzgerald. "I hope his overall game didn't plummet in order for his physical prowess to take effect these past few years."

"That is possible, but I do feel the ability to regain a role inside the top nine may be some inspiration for James," announced GM Flaherty.

"And Harrison?" asked Coach Fitzgerald.

Assistant GM Chambers took a sip of coffee and leaned forward in his chair. "Gage was able to get some exposure last year in a top-six role in Junior B as an underage player. For anyone that has seen him play, they consider him one of the most intriguing players to come from the local system. He has a high skill level and could blend very well with Kip on the first line. He also has his history of playing with Turcotte from their minor hockey days, so he should be a perfect fit on one of our top-scoring lines."

"Great! Good to hear," said Coach Fitzgerald. "Now the two D we have signed: Freeman and Black?"

"Yes," said Assistant GM Chambers. "Well, Dallas Freeman and Wallace Black will be the anchors of this team—in my opinion. Both have played Major Junior and are well-sized—and that is an understatement for Black. Freeman carries himself strongly all over the ice and is a very solid contributor at both ends of the rink. Black—at 6'5" and 200-plus pounds—is a force to be reckoned with. He plays a physical game, but within the boundaries of the rules. Not a player I would want to engage with."

"Beautiful," said Coach Fitzgerald. "I have to say, the base of the team has come along very nicely. I look forward to building around these guys!"

"And finally, in net we have Carter Riddle," Assistant GM carried on. "An experienced goaltender in this league, who will be able to provide some stability while we work with one of the younger options in a backup role."

"Carter is from the area, as well?" asked Coach Fitzgerald.

"Yes, he played with Kelley, Northgate and Freeman, actually," responded GM Flaherty. "They were the cornerstones of their team's successes—much like the group of Roberts, Martinson, Sharp and Nectle this past season for their AAA team."

"Nectle's the goalie right?" asked Coach Fitzgerald. "What's he like?"

GM Flaherty and Assistant GM Chambers looked at each other to see who should express their input on Sam Nectle—GM Flaherty decided to take the lead.

"Well, Sammy isn't the biggest goalie at 5'11", but he is rarely out of position and is very reliable. I am looking forward to seeing how he does with us, but another year in midget or finding a Junior B or C team may be the best option for him this season."

Coach Fitzgerald nodded. "I guess there will be many variables in the upcoming weeks regarding the team."

The Revolution staff continued with their meeting, discussing a variety of topics that needed to be addressed involving the team and the progression of training camp.

CHAPTER III

ON THE WAY

Main Street was quiet as DJ and his father, Bryan Roberts, drove south down the roadway and made their way to Memorial Arena. The drive took approximately ten minutes to complete on a day like today, and the father-and-son duo were able to have a brief discussion before arriving at the arena.

"How are you feeling this morning? Get enough sleep?" questioned Mr. Roberts.

"Feeling great!" responded DJ.

"Ready to go?"

"Absolutely!" replied DJ confidently, with a smile.

"Feeling any pressure?"

"To be honest…" and DJ thought about it for a moment, "not overly. I understand what this day means, but I know— and I trust—my ability. I don't want to sound conceited, but this is the moment I've been working for over the last few months. I am ready to go!"

His dad nodded. "Now, I understand your confidence— and I am not downplaying your skill level—but be ready to work. This is what you have been focused on—without a doubt! But don't forget what got you here: hard work, perseverance and determination! If you come to work, you won't leave with any regrets."

"I know…" DJ replied automatically. DJ knew his dad wasn't trying to apply additional pressure on him, but just trying to instill the proper values in him.

Mr. Roberts took the next left turn and entered the Memorial Arena parking lot. He crept along the drive and circled around toward the front entrance. DJ got out and opened the back door to get his hockey bag and sticks.

"Thanks for the ride, Dad!"

"No problem, son. Good luck! We will be up in the stands supporting you!"

"Thanks! See you later," DJ responded as he swung the door shut and made his way to the entrance.

As he entered the building he was greeted by a familiar face.

"Hey, DJ!" It was Marty, who had arrived just moments ahead of his friend. "Ready to go today?"

"Yeah," DJ responded in a surprised tone. "Why are you here so early, buddy?"

Marty laughed. "They're doing physicals ahead of the skates, plus I wanted to see my competition! So, thought I would get here and check things out early!"

"Fair enough!"

"Dropped off my bag at the room—they have the lineups posted on the doors. You are playing with Kip Kelley! Dozer is on your right side."

Dozer was the nickname for Joel Stevenson. Stevenson was a year older than DJ and Marty, but they were all very good friends. The hulking 6'3" winger earned his nickname from his gritty play and power-forward style of hockey. Dozer always found his way to the net, whether he had an open lane or had to "bulldoze" his way through his opponents.

"Really?" responded DJ enthusiastically. "Kip Kelley is actually coming back to play?"

"Yeah," answered Marty. "Was talking to Kole the other day. Said that he went back up for the camp there and wasn't really keen on staying. So, he decided to ask for his release and come back home to play."

"Wow! That is a big pickup!"

"Kole was pretty pumped," Marty continued. "He trained a lot this off-season with Kipper and feels good coming into camp—he desperately wants to play with him."

Kole Kelley was Kip's younger brother and chummed around with DJ and Marty quite frequently. He was the same age as Dozer and the two had played many years of hockey together. Kole held his brother in high regard and tried to emulate his own game after him. While he wasn't quite as naturally gifted as Kip, he had certainly earned his opportunity to compete for a position with the Revolution.

"Well, hopefully he is able to show off what he is capable of this weekend," stated DJ. "That would be pretty awesome for them to play together." DJ took a quick glance up at the clock in the main lobby, "I suppose I should head down to do the physical—talk to you later, dude!"

"Good luck out there!" said Marty as he gave him a friendly nudge on the shoulder.

DJ carried on down the corridor to the dressing rooms. As he walked through the hallway he couldn't help but think of what a great opportunity he was being given to line up next to Kip Kelley. Kip was well known by all of the players in their age bracket and someone they all admired. During the summers, DJ had been able to get to know him slightly, as Kip was part of the group of players that would assemble at the arena for a weekly skate.

At Memorial Arena, the Revolution had been able to come to an agreement with town council to add an addition to the building for their very own dressing room. The nearly-$400,000 project was state-of-the-art and included personal stalls for the players, a management office, coaches' office, trainer's room and meeting room/kitchen—all the amenities of any professional or well-established junior hockey team. DJ got to the Revolution's dressing room door and took a deep breath. After dropping his bag along the wall in the hallway, he entered the room. As he made his way into the space, he was greeted with smiles from the Revolution staff members as he entered the office area.

"DJ!" announced GM Flaherty proudly. "Good morning, buddy!"

"Good morning Mr. Flaherty. I just assumed that we were doing physicals in the team room?"

"Yes! You're early and have some time, so why don't you come on in and I can introduce you to the coaching staff."

"Great!" said DJ.

Mr. Flaherty motioned toward his staff, "First, our head coach—a man I know you are well aware of—Mr. Steve Fitzgerald. Next in line are Assistant Coaches Larry McIntosh and Craig Horton." DJ stood up from his seat and shook hands with all three members of the coaching staff. "And of course, my right-hand man, Assistant GM Doug Chambers." DJ proceeded to shake hands with Mr. Chambers as well before returning to his seat just inside the door of the office.

"I'm glad you are here early, DJ," announced Coach Fitzgerald. "Not sure if you came across the lineup we posted for the day, but I am expecting big things from you and want to see what you can do next to Kip Kelley."

"Actually," DJ started, "I didn't see it—however Brad Martinsen met me in the lobby as I came in and told me all about it. I'm very excited for this opportunity!"

"Marty is here already? Doesn't surprise me one bit that you two are the first in the building," said Mr. Flaherty.

"Yeah, he's ready to go! We've been looking forward to this for quite some time," said DJ.

"Indeed!" Mr. Flaherty smiled. "As we all have! Anyway, I'll have you slide back to the trainer's room to meet with Dr. Andrews. He'll take care of your physical and then you are free to prepare for the first skate."

DJ said his farewells to the men in the office and made his way over to see Dr. Jim Andrews. Dr. Andrews was a local physiotherapist and very well respected in the community. DJ was familiar with Dr. Andrews both as a client and as a friend to the physiotherapist's son and daughter. Joshua Andrews was a year younger than DJ and the two knew each other through hockey and school. Dr. Andrews' daughter, Rebecca, had grown up with DJ and been in the same class as him since they had started kindergarten.

"Morning, Dr. Andrews," greeted DJ as he entered the trainer's room.

"Well, if it isn't young Mr. Roberts," replied Dr. Andrews. "Early and ready to go!"

"Yes sir!"

"Great, let's have a quick little examination here and get you on your way."

Dr. Andrews recorded DJ's height and weight, and then proceeded to carry on with his examination to ensure DJ was in good standing physically before hitting the ice.

"Well, young sir," Dr. Andrews stated, "all appears to be in good condition for you. Good luck out there this morning!"

"Thanks, Dr. Andrews."

After the examination, DJ left the trainer's room and exited the Revolution's locker room altogether. He then picked up his equipment and headed toward the dressing rooms where the players would be getting ready during the training camp. DJ was normally a very calm person, but he could feel his heart rate increasing and a fluttering in his stomach as he anticipated the first skate of the camp.

CHAPTER IV

ΠAVY HITS THE ICE

Over the last half hour, the players had been steadily gathering in Dressing Room Four as DJ prepared himself for the morning ice session with Team Navy. Finally, after several familiar and not-so-familiar faces had entered the room, Joel Stevenson emerged through the door. Dozer made his way directly over to DJ, carrying a smile on his face the entire way.

"DJ, my man!"

"Good to see you, Dozer," replied DJ.

"Okay line… I suppose," Dozer said modestly.

DJ laughed. "Yeah, not too bad, eh!?"

"You ready to go, or what?" questioned DJ's big friend.

"Too ready, maybe. This morning couldn't come quick enough. I just want to get out on the ice and forget about all this anticipation."

Dozer nodded in agreement. "Completely understand, my man! Let's make our presence be known."

DJ and Dozer began to get their gear on and continued with the small talk among themselves and a few of the others in the room. DJ always enjoyed getting completely dressed before he allowed himself a chance to sit and take in the moment, so when he finished throwing on his practice jersey, he gazed around the room. He knew many of the players around him and he noted the ones that were new to him. He wondered what their backgrounds were, and he made snap judgements on who he thought would be interesting to see on the ice.

One familiar player he noticed was James Northgate. DJ knew that Northgate had—like Kip Kelley—come back from playing Major Junior hockey and was very intrigued with what the big-bodied winger would be able to accomplish with the Revolution this season. DJ noticed a second player who seemed really engaged in the conversations happening around the room, but whose manner was somewhat reserved.

"Hey, Dozer," DJ began. "Any idea who that is over there, beside Northgate?"

Dozer glanced up from tying his skate. "Umm… I think that's Dominic O'Connor. Played junior hockey up around the Georgian Bay area, I believe."

"Oh yeah?"

"Pretty sure. Think he's going to school here now. Taking a business course or something like that."

"Seems like a decent guy," replied DJ.

DJ continued to take in the atmosphere of the dressing room as he waited patiently for the clock to strike 10:00 am. Just then, Assistant Coach Larry McIntosh entered the room carrying a clipboard.

"Morning gentlemen, I'm Assistant Coach Larry McIntosh. I will be working with Team Navy during training camp. I just wanted to come in and introduce myself and go over a few things that we are going to do this morning."

All of the players paid close attention to Coach McIntosh as he continued. "First, let me go through the lineup for line rushes and for the game this afternoon." He worked his way through the lineup and informed the goalies that they would each be given a period during the intersquad game. "For further information, check out the page on the door."

<u>Line Combinations</u>

<u>Team Navy</u>
<u>Forwards</u>
DJ Roberts – Kip Kelley – Joel Stevenson
Dominic O'Connor – Stewart Cooke – James Northgate
Cam Zalapski – Nolan Anderson – Nathan Anderson
Levi Provolie – Brendan Burrow – Chase Livermore

<u>Defence</u>
Wallace Black – Curtis Kraemer
Andrew Boersman – Martin Killington
Dave Gillies – Donald Redman

<u>Goalies</u>
Edward Boushy
Sam Nectle
Spencer McIntyre

Coach McIntosh flipped to the next page on his clipboard. "So, on the ice today, we'll run a few shooting drills to warm up the goalies and get the legs and hands going. Then we will break off and do some 2-on-1s and 3-on-2s before finishing off with some breakout and transition drills."

Coach McIntosh looked up and around the room at the group. "Both squads will be running through the same drills so we can get a comparison on how everyone is handling the practice. But more importantly, it is for you to hone your skills so you are sharp heading into the intersquad game this afternoon. Are there questions?"

The players remained silent and glanced around at each other—as if to say, "I am aware of what is being asked of me. Are you?"

"Good! Well guys, this is the moment you've been waiting for. I would like to be the first to welcome you to training camp, and to wish you all the best of luck going forward. See you on the ice!" Coach McIntosh vacated the room and allowed the players to finish getting ready.

DJ and Dozer both threw on their helmets and gloves and got up from the bench simultaneously. They walked toward the door of the dressing room and picked up their sticks from where they were leaning against the wall.

"Here we go, DJ!" Dozer said as he held up a fist. DJ gave him a fist bump and the two linemates left the room.

As he hit the ice, DJ was met by cool, refreshing air as he began to skate counter-clockwise around the arena. He skated beside Dozer and the two stretched out and warmed up their legs. A few laps in, the two were joined by defencemen Andrew Boersman and Dave Gillies. Boersman had played with Dozer last season and was a very physical hockey player. His aggressive style often lead to penalties, but he drew the admiration of his teammates as he would stand up for them in all situations. His counterpart, Dave Gillies, was a smaller defenceman with good hockey instincts. Gillies was another underage player and had played with DJ and Marty last season.

"Dozer!" shouted Boersman as he skated up beside the two forwards. "You ready to cause some havoc today, or what?"

Dozer laughed. "Yeah, man! Have to make an impact somehow!"

"I hear you, buddy!" said Boersman as he laughed along. "Gills here was saying you are all but signed, DJ! That's pretty awesome, man!"

DJ downplayed the remark. "I'm out here to make a case for myself, that's all. Nothing is a guarantee. There's lots of talent out here."

Gillies spoke up, "Yeah, but there is no way you aren't on the team, bud! So…"

DJ smiled. "We'll see. Let's focus on winning the game today and let things play out accordingly."

"Always so humble!" said Gillies.

"Alright, boys," Boersman carried on. "Let's do this!"

While the players chatted and joked around, Coach McIntosh arrived on the ice and blew his whistle to halt the circulating players and call them to centre ice.

The players went through the various drills that they were instructed to complete. The line rushes allowed everyone to get warmed up and by the time the 2-on-1 and 3-on-2 rushes began, DJ was feeling good and in the groove. He focused on himself, but he was a keen watcher and took note of what the other players were doing, as well.

From the lineup, he watched as Kip Kelley and O'Connor took on Gillies in the first 2-on-1. Kip and O'Connor worked the puck back and forth quickly. Gillies closed the gap slightly as they moved up the ice and Kip held onto the puck between the two bluelines. As a right-handed shot, he protected the puck far away from the defender as he skated on the outside. Once the two attackers hit the blueline, O'Connor put on a burst of speed and darted in on Edward Boushy in net. Kip attacked with poise and waited for the ideal moment to send a six-inch saucer pass to O'Connor for a tap-in goal.

DJ turned to Dozer, "Wow! That was impressive."

"No doubt," Dozer replied.

DJ and Dozer were up next. The two moved out of the zone toward Wallace Black on defence. The big defenceman wasn't the fastest skater, but he used his size and strong stick positioning to take away time and space effectively. DJ gathered up a pass on the inside as they crossed the redline. DJ immediately broke to the outside and tried to press Black with his speed—this allowed Dozer to open up for a one-time opportunity as he moved into the high slot. DJ attempted a quick backhand drop pass, but the experienced defenceman was able to stop the scoring threat with ease.

"Sorry, dude! I've got to make that play," declared DJ as they headed to the corner.

"No worries," responded Dozer. "Good defensive play by Blacky."

DJ continued watching in anticipation of his next opportunity. He took in the Andersons, who were able to break down the defenders with slick offensive plays. Then once again he watched Kelley and O'Connor dazzle as they took on Black this time. The more DJ watched O'Connor, the more impressed he was.

"I really like how O'Connor plays," he said to Dozer as they waited in line.

"Seems to mesh well with Kipper," replied Dozer.

The two were back up and set to take on Boersman this time. The forwards broke out into the neutral zone and DJ broke to the outside once again. Boersman—not quite as positionally sound as Black—couldn't maintain his position on DJ as he buzzed by. Dozer became obsolete as DJ broke in all alone on Sam Nectle. Nectle bit on a quick shoulder dip, and DJ sent a hard snap shot over the goalie's right shoulder and into the net.

"Beauty goal, DJ!" said Dozer as they returned to the corner. "No chance for Drew or Sammy there."

"Thanks, buddy!"

DJ gained confidence after scoring the goal and carried on with some swagger for the remaining portion of the morning skate. He felt good following the session and had a better idea of what to expect from his teammates heading into the afternoon. In his mind, he went over a few players that he was intrigued by. Kip Kelley was an obvious standout, but he also thought Dominic O'Connor, James Northgate, Wallace Black and Curtis Kraemer were outstanding. Kraemer was a very offensive-minded defenceman. Last season he had been an underage player in the local Junior C loop. He had posted very strong numbers and seemed poised to progress his game to the next level.

As they left the ice and headed to the dressing room, DJ said to Dozer, "Well, that was fun! Looking forward to this afternoon."

"Same here," replied the big right winger.

CHAPTER V

THE ACTION FROM ABOVE

Bryan and Susie Roberts watched the morning skate from up in the stands, alongside Marty and his parents, Bill and Patty Martinsen. The group talked about how exciting the upcoming season would be if both DJ and Marty were able to make the Revolution. About halfway through the first skate, Marty left to get ready. The parents carried on their conversation and took in the remaining portion of Team Navy's on-ice session.

"DJ has looked really strong, so far," declared Bill.

"He has played well," agreed Bryan. "They've been open about giving the boys plenty of opportunity to prove themselves, so it's good to see."

"Quite a number of underage players in competition with them," said Bill.

Bryan nodded. "Yes. From my recollection, there are about 12 underage skaters and three goaltenders. Probably six or seven with a viable chance for the two available cards..."

"And who knows who could become available—someone released from Major Junior or a different team," added Bill.

"True," responded Bryan.

"But, if they already sign the two underage cards available, are they filled for the season regardless of those other factors?" questioned Patty.

"I believe once a card is signed it can no longer be used on any other skater," replied Bryan. "That's my understanding, anyway."

"Well, let's hope our boys snag those spots as soon as possible," exclaimed Patty.

"Indeed," agreed Susie.

The foursome continued to watch as the first skate came to an end, and they remained in their seats as Team Silver went out onto the ice. They watched Marty hit the ice and warm up—much like DJ and Team Navy had done one hour prior. It wasn't long before DJ joined the parents up in the stands, filling the seat Marty had left when he went to get ready.

"Hi, guys," DJ said as he sat down.

"Hey, DJ," they said in unison.

"Great work out there this morning," Bill continued.

"Yes, nice work son," DJ's parents agreed.

"Thanks," DJ replied. "Looks like I didn't miss too much action out there."

"Nope, they are just starting into the warm-up drills," answered his dad.

All eyes returned to the action on the ice. Team Silver had some talented players working hard to impress the Revolution staff gathered roughly 100 feet from where the Roberts and Martinsens were seated. DJ saw that all the members were equipped with clipboards and plenty of paperwork. He observed GM Flaherty and Coach Fitzgerald deep in conversation, all the while intently watching the practice happening before them. They periodically would motion to a play on the ice, and then refer to their notes—adding to them or reviewing information accordingly.

On the ice, Team Silver had started into 2-on-1s and DJ couldn't help but notice—and cheer on—his best friend as he took part in the drill. Marty lined up with Mike McDennis. Their pairing was fitting, as the two of them had lined up with DJ all year long and they had created a dynamic threesome. Mike brought grit and played a tenacious style of game that helped create open areas for his two skilled linemates. Mike's ability to generate scoring space for his linemates also led to his own offensive success, as he finished the season second in goals.

Marty and Mike moved up the ice rapidly. Marty started on the inside and quickly used his agility and acceleration to force the defenceman in a crossing pattern leading toward the offensive blueline. Marty was unbelievable at executing his lateral movement and made it very hard for defenders to manage. At only 5 feet and 7 inches, he worked with a small frame, but rarely got caught in any physical engagements with his opponents as he weaved his way through traffic effortlessly.

As Marty moved in across the blueline, Mike made an effort to get to the front of the net. The defenceman played the two perfectly and took away a direct pass—or so he thought. Marty quickly looked up and fed a pass through the defender's legs and Mike was able to control it well enough to get a decent scoring chance out of the play. As he cradled the pass, Mike took a glance up and aimed for the five-hole; however, goalie Carter Riddle read the play beautifully and shut it down with a stick save.

"Great chance, guys!" shouted Patty Martinsen from the crowd.

DJ couldn't fight off the grin that came onto his face. Watching his former linemates brought back great memories from last season. Unfortunately for the fabulous line, with only two cards available, they wouldn't have a chance to replicate that success this season with the Revolution.

GM Flaherty and Coach Fitzgerald conversed for nearly the entire duration of both skates. They analyzed the players that stood out, whether it was for good or bad reasons. As Team Silver's skate closed out, the two started to walk back down to the office.

"Well, Coach," started GM Flaherty, "looks like a lot of talent to choose from out there."

"I liked what I saw," said Coach Fitzgerald. "We have a lot of skilled, young players. My only concern is that when we strip away all of the underage players in camp, will we have enough depth and selection to fill out our lineup?"

"That is a valid concern," concurred Mr. Flaherty. "I assure you that Doug and I are working hard at attracting suitable players in our direction—it's a process. We just need to be patient for the time-being."

"If the season were to start today, I feel I would be able to ice a competitive squad. So, I can be tolerant… for now." The two stopped outside GM Flaherty's office. "I will see you later on after lunch."

GM Flaherty entered the office as he and Coach Fitzgerald parted ways. He walked to his desk and picked up the phone, dialed and waited calmly for an answer on the other end. "Good day, Jim. Bob Flaherty here—how are you?" Mr. Flaherty waited for the response. "So, any news on upcoming releases?"

CHAPTER VI

ΠΑVY AND SILVER GAME #1

The Roberts and Martinsens all met up at The Subhouse—a local sandwich shop and favourite stop to eat at between DJ's and Marty's summer workouts. The two families had spent a lot of time together over the last several years as the boys travelled across Ontario—and even into other provinces and the United States—for their hockey. Their AAA team had gone as far as Quebec to the north, Massachusetts to the east, Minnesota to the west and Ohio to the south to compete in tournaments; trips that included up to 12 hours of driving.

As everyone ate their sub, the chatter—as usual—surrounded hockey and the upcoming game in the afternoon. DJ and Marty ribbed each other and placed a friendly wager on the outcome. The loser would have to wear the other's favourite hockey team's jersey to their first day back at school. It wasn't a daunting task, nevertheless the two competitive hockey players didn't want to end up on the wrong side of the bet. The group finished eating and got into their vehicles to return to the arena. It was closing in on 2:00 pm, leaving the guys around an hour to get ready for the clash on the ice.

As they walked toward the arena doors, DJ and Marty walked stride for stride. They entered the building together and headed down toward the dressing rooms.

"Well," said DJ, "I guess this is where we part ways, dude!"

"Good luck, man," responded Marty. And the two friends shook hands.

"You too!"

Marty entered Dressing Room One, while DJ continued down to Dressing Room Four. In their respective dressing rooms, each went through their customary pre-game rituals. In DJ's case, he grabbed both of his sticks and brought them over to his hockey bag. Reaching into his bag, he retrieved a smaller, black bag where he kept his tape and extra odds and ends. He pulled out a roll of white tape and a pair of scissors. He proceeded to peel the tape off the blade of the stick he had used in the morning and began to put a fresh layer back on, taping it right down to the toe of the blade. He then used his scissors to trim off the excess tape at the toe of the stick.

He dressed, then sat and visualized the upcoming game, anticipating what plays might happen and how he would go about handling them. He envisioned breaking out on his strong-side wing and receiving a breakaway pass. After taking the pass, he looked up and saw the goaltender challenging him. DJ cocked his stick as if he were going to release a quick wrist shot, then made a hard move to his backhand and around the sprawled out goalie—burying the puck inside the gaping net.

Every member of Team Navy had a similar mental state; the team was focused and quiet. They got ready silently and before long, Coach McIntosh arrived to offer some words of encouragement.

"Alright, guys," he started. "Very good skate this morning. I'm hoping you felt better as it went along and are ready to bring a strong effort this afternoon. This is your first chance to really show us what you can bring to the Revolution this year. Make a case for yourself. We have a lot of youth in this room and many of you will be around this team over the next few years, whether you make it this season or not. Having said that, make it hard for us to not keep you on the main roster right out of the gate!"

He took a quick break and looked over the paper on his clipboard. "We'll be keeping the same lines as this morning. For tomorrow, I assume the majority of you will likely remain on Team Navy, but if any changes are made to the lineup then you will be contacted this evening." He paused and put his clipboard to his side. "Okay, guys, unless there are any questions, we're ready to go. Kelley's line will start with Black and Kraemer on the point; Boushy in net for period one. Let's go have some fun, boys!"

Coach McIntosh left the room and the players threw on their remaining equipment. DJ tossed on his helmet and gloves, then picked up his stick and got up from his seat.

"Let's go here now!" hollered Kip Kelley. "This is what we've been waiting for."

Kip's comments seemed to ease the tension in the room and the guys were more vocal as they walked down the hall and onto the ice; Team Silver joined them shortly after at the other end. The players on both sides did a few laps before breaking off into their respective corners to warm up the goaltenders with a few shots. The warm-up was brief and before long the official blew his whistle to signify the end. DJ, Kip Kelley and Dozer remained on the ice and huddled near centre.

"Alright, guys. Let's keep it simple to start. Get our legs going and get some pressure on them down low," stated Kip. DJ and Dozer nodded in agreement. "Keep the talk alive out here!"

The huddle split up and they aligned themselves for the opening faceoff. Kip circled in and met his opposition with a smile. JJ Turcotte was his counterpart on the draw and the two prepared for the referee to drop the puck. With a quick flip of his wrist, the ref released the puck from his hand and officially began the game.

Kip and JJ swung their sticks simultaneously, with Kip receiving a favourable bounce off his blade and allowing Team Navy to gain control. The puck dribbled in behind his feet and DJ quickly left his post on the left side to poke the puck back to Wallace Black on defence. Black backtracked with the puck, allowing his teammates to move into motion and open up some passing lanes. He had some immediate pressure from Harrison Gage, forcing him to make a cross-ice pass to Curtis Kraemer. Kraemer one-touched the puck into the middle and Kip took control of it and turned up ice.

Kip skated with the puck and quickly flipped a saucer pass to the wall—where Dozer held position at Team Silver's blueline. Dozer didn't waste any time and dumped the puck in behind the defence. This gave DJ an opportunity to press Dallas Freeman in the corner. Freeman felt the pressure on his left shoulder and rimmed the puck around to the weak side where Matt Manson of Team Silver retrieved it.

Manson attempted an outlet pass, but the adept Kip Kelley snuck in to break up the dish and regained possession for Team Navy. Kip glanced up as he turned toward the goal and saw his big right winger driving the net. With a flick of the wrist, Kip sent a hard pass in the direction of Dozer's stick—looking for a redirect on net. Dozer realized the intent of the play and tipped the puck in an effort for a goal. The puck was met swiftly by Carter Riddle's left pad, as he kicked it out on the redirection. It bounced off Riddle's pad and out to the right corner.

DJ, who had pressed Freeman in the corner just seconds ago, was still in the vicinity and took control of the puck once again. Feeling some pressure from the defenders, he bounced a pass to Curtis Kraemer off the sidewall. Kraemer picked up the pass and used some skillful foot work to move across the blueline and release a hard, low shot on net. Riddle once again was there to meet the shot, but this time he tracked it with his glove and snagged the puck out of the air—holding on for a whistle. Team Navy circled around and showed their approval for the combined efforts on the play.

"Great work!" communicated Kip Kelley as he came together with DJ and Dozer.

"Nice try, boys," added Black from the blueline.

The line moved in for the offensive zone faceoff, but they were unable to gain control of the draw and Team Silver was able to break out of their zone. The play balanced out over the next few shifts, with neither team able to move into any quality scoring areas. DJ, Kip and Dozer returned to the ice for their second shift, but they were unable to muster more than a few perimeter shots—all leading to a quick change of possession and loss of offensive zone time.

A few minutes later, Team Silver was able to secure an offensive zone faceoff and that led to Marty's line coming out onto the ice. DJ watched as his best friend took action. Marty—lined up with Mike McDennis and another local player named Anson Brown—was able to win the ensuing faceoff back to McDennis, who was positioned on the boards. McDennis took a hard stride out to the middle of the ice and fired a shot in the direction of the goal. Brown held his position out in the slot and tied up the defender, creating a screen on goaltender Edward Boushy. Boushy saw the shot at the last second and flung his body to the left in an effort to block the shot from entering the goal. His effort was successful, but it led to a rebound that met the stick of the attacking centre. Marty was able to pull the puck onto his backhand and around the goaltender, creating a wide open cage to score on—he fired a backhand shot into the net to make the score 1–0 for Team Silver.

His linemates quickly engaged with him to celebrate before they returned to centre ice for the next faceoff. DJ and his line were called upon by Coach McIntosh, and they headed over the boards. As DJ skated to his position on the wing, he glanced over at Marty. Marty gave him a wink on the way by.

"Nice one, Marty," DJ complimented his friend. "Next one's mine though!"

Marty gave him a nod and then returned his focus to the draw. Kip and Marty clashed together as the puck plummeted to the ice. Marty—always a crafty faceoff man—was able to kick the puck back toward Victor Sharp. Sharp gathered up the puck and made a D-to-D pass to his partner, Matthew MacKenzie. The defenceman gained the redline and dumped the puck hard into the offensive zone. Team Silver swarmed on the forecheck, but Kip Kelley was able to create a turnover and poke the puck out to Dozer on the right side.

"Yup… yup," called out DJ as he broke across the ice in support.

Dozer sent him a pass and DJ immediately broke out on the flat-footed defender. Sharp made an effort to steal the puck back at the blueline, but DJ was able to dodge the check and continued his rush. MacKenzie skated hard and took away a clean breakaway from the left winger. The two engaged in a one-on-one and DJ drove the defender back toward Team Silver's goal before hitting the brakes and opening up into a shooting position. On the move, DJ was able to create some space.

"DJ... whoop, whoop!" shouted Kip as he flew up the ice behind DJ and into a prime scoring area.

DJ saw Kip enter the frame and made a quick dish to the centreman. Kip was open and ready to one-time the pass, but a stick moved into the lane and deflected the puck into the corner. Marty had tracked Kip all the way back from the other end and made an impressive defensive effort to break up the scoring opportunity. Team Silver once again ended the chance of any scoring threat from the Kelley line, as they took control of the puck and relieved themselves from any sustained pressure.

"Where in the world did Marty come from?" howled Kip as they returned to the bench.

"He's always been a persistent backchecker," said DJ. "Never quits on a play!"

"I guess not!" said Kip as he punched the boards in frustration.

The play continued at a quick pace for the remaining portion of the first period. Team Navy wasn't able to gain much from their efforts on offence, but Team Silver capitalized on a late-period goal off JJ Turcotte's stick—bringing their lead to 2–0 heading into intermission.

The players all vacated the ice as the Zamboni came out to clean it between play. Team Navy's dressing room was quiet, once again. Each player knew they had to bring their personal game to a higher level entering the new period, and they displayed a quiet self-assurance as they got up from their seats to return to the ice.

The teams came out and started the second stanza with an elevated intensity. Team Silver was able to gain a bit of momentum to begin the period and they tested Sam Nectle early on. Nectle was set to Matt Murphy in Team Silver's net. The two netminders were used to this matchup, having been engaged in this altercation numerous times over their AAA tenures.

The two goalies were involved in a sequence of back-and-forth action, leading to many incredible and systematic stops in the process. In one particular play, Nectle was in the midst of a frantic scrum in front of his net that saw him turn away three great scoring opportunities. Team Navy seemed to rally based on his stellar performance and were able to press up the ice offensively on the next play.

The line made up of Dominic O'Connor, Stewart Cooke and James Northgate hemmed Team Silver in their own zone and cycled the puck deep, wearing down the defenders. O'Connor gathered up the puck from the corner and pivoted as he skated out toward the blueline. He once again passed the puck down low to Northgate—then bolted into the slot.

In the corner, Northgate gained possession of the puck on his forehand. He heard O'Connor calling for a return pass as he broke into the gap. Northgate slung a pass into the middle and O'Connor took control on his backhand. In one swift motion, he brought the puck across his body and released a quick snap shot along the ice—the shot beat Murphy between the legs to bring Team Navy within a goal.

Team Navy's bench erupted as the puck entered the net and the spark seemed to ignite the players as a whole. Their immediate shifts following the goal were seemingly played on a downhill slope as they pressed Team Silver on their half of the ice.

DJ, Kip and Dozer hopped onto the ice as part of an on-the-fly change and formed into a 1-2 forecheck. Kip held the middle of the ice and guided the puck carrier to DJ on the left side. DJ stepped up, was able to strip the puck away and feed it to Kip as he curled back toward the offensive zone. Kip broke wide on the defence tandem of Shayne Purves and Cody Ryerson and drove them deep into their zone. Dozer charged into the slot to support Kip, but Kip saw an opportunity unfolding behind the immediate action. Curtis Kraemer had jumped into the play and was wide open in the high slot, and Kip made no mistake in his pass. Kraemer retrieved the puck all alone, 30 feet out from the goal and took his time to gain control and pick his spot. With a hard and accurate wrist shot, Kraemer beat Matt Murphy's glove to tie the game at 2–2.

The players on the bench jumped up in celebration as the offensive defenceman buried the goal. Kraemer immediately sought out the playmaker who made the goal viable, and he gave Kip a celebratory hug. As the period moved along, Navy continued to elevate their play, but they were unable to take a lead as the period came to a close.

"Great period, guys," stated Kip as he stood at the gate, high-fiving the players as they left the ice for the second intermission. This was an accurate statement, as Team Navy not only scored twice, but had also outshot the Silver squad 16-to-6 throughout the period.

Coach McIntosh made sure to let the team know that their effort hadn't gone unnoticed—he stepped into the dressing room to congratulate them on their work. "Great period," he started. "Let's try to bring that same intensity in the third and pick up the win, guys."

The players knew that the end result of the game wasn't truly important, however, they couldn't deny their instinctive habit of always wanting to come out on the winning side. While the first and second periods were filled with some intense moments, the third period was at its climax from the beginning. Both teams knew that this was their final chance to make an impression on the first day of camp.

The Kelley line started the period once again. They faced off against the combination of Marty, Brown and McDennis. The two lines set the stage when they brought some end-to-end action to the early moments of the period. Neither team managed to gain much in terms of quality scoring opportunities, but the pace was rapid and this continued as the next lines took the ice. The players' determination was evident as the period progressed, but neither side was willing to break.

At the midway point of the period, DJ hopped on the ice in advance of his linemates to relieve a winded Levi Provolie. Brendan Burrow and Chase Livermore were ahead of the action and applying some pressure on the Team Silver defencemen. The two underage forwards made it difficult for the Silver squad to get a clean breakout. Eventually, the big-bodied Burrow delivered a massive bodycheck on Shayne Purves and picked up the puck deep in the offensive zone. DJ read the play and came into a gap in the high slot.

"Yeah… yeah!" DJ yelled as he entered the scoring zone.

Burrow, with his head up, saw DJ call for it and sent out a hard pass. DJ cradled the puck and released a blistering shot past the outstretched glove of third period goaltender, David Powers. DJ greeted Burrow with a high-five as the two met in the corner.

"Great work," DJ said to both Burrow and Livermore as they celebrated.

"Nice shot, DJ," said Chase Livermore to his former AAA captain.

DJ cycled back to centre ice and was joined by his regular linemates. Off the draw, Kip managed to take control and immediately pressed in on the Team Silver defence. Kip toe dragged the puck away from Dallas Freeman's stick, then proceeded to slide the puck between his own legs and split the defensive pairing in one motion—leading to a breakaway. Kip closed in on the net and sent a quick shot into the feet of the goalie. Powers didn't expect the quick release and dropped into a butterfly, but he couldn't close the gap in time. The quick strike brought Team Navy's lead to 4–2—only eight seconds after taking the lead.

The players raced over to congratulate the spectacular play by the star centre.

"Whoo!" screeched Dozer as he picked up Kip in a bear hug.

"That was unbelievable," announced DJ as he came in for a high-five.

Kip just chuckled as he received the admiration from his linemates.

The Kelley goal took the wind out of Team Silver's sails. With Team Navy's four unanswered goals holding firm until the final minutes of the period, Marty earned his team a power play with some tenacious play down low in the offensive zone. Marty remained on the ice, and was joined by JJ Turcotte's line, Eric Matheson and Dallas Freeman. Team Silver now took a 6-on-4 advantage as they tried to close the deficit in the dying moments of the intersquad game.

Marty came in for the offensive zone faceoff and won it cleanly back to Freeman on the back end. Freeman walked the blueline, but Team Navy's penalty kill didn't allow him a chance to fire one toward the net. Instead, Freeman slid the puck back in the direction that he had come from. JJ Turcotte, who moved into the open ice Freeman had created, picked up the puck and watched the play unfold as he remained unforced.

Marty worked himself in off the backside of the goaltender and he was left uncontested. Marty waved his stick—to signal that he wanted the puck—and Turcotte fired a pass through the seam in his direction. Marty gained control and was immediately pressured by Wallace Black— who skated away his man out front of the net. Marty beat Black's stick check and fed the puck to Harrison Gage in front of the net. Gage sliced the puck up and over the shoulder of third period goaltender, Spencer McIntyre. The goal stopped the clock at 1:33, in what was now a 4–3 hockey game.

The same six players remained on the ice for Team Silver—and they were energized. Coach McIntosh knew he needed to return to his power line, so he tapped Kip Kelley on the shoulder.

"Shut them down, guys," Coach McIntosh said as he sent the Kelley line over the boards.

DJ looked up at his coach and nodded. "Will do, Coach!"

The trio returned to the ice and lined up against their opposition. Kip faced off with Marty—and lost. Freeman took control of the puck and took a few hard strides up ice before chipping it high over the heads of Team Navy on a cross-ice dump.

Wallace Black charged back to retrieve the puck, but he was met by the forechecking tandem of Matt Manson and JJ Turcotte. Manson engaged in physical play with Black, while

Turcotte took control of the puck. As he gained possession, Turcotte buttonhooked up the wall and slid the puck back to Freeman at the blueline.

DJ closed in on Freeman and took away the shooting lane—forcing a dump into the corner. Marty trapped the puck on the wall and protected the puck away from the pressure applied by Curtis Kraemer. Turcotte moved along the wall and criss-crossed with Marty as he skated out of the corner. The young centre delivered a drop pass to Turcotte, allowing him to skate into uncontested ice.

Turcotte had a few seconds to scan the ice and saw Harrison Gage creeping in off the backside of the goaltender. Without hesitation, Turcotte sent a quick saucer pass cross-crease in Gage's direction. The pass landed perfectly and Gage sat poised to one-time the puck into the open net, but Kip lifted Gage's stick at the last possible moment and spoiled the chance.

The puck skipped all the way across to the far wall, where Dozer was able to scoop it up and clear the zone with a high loft. DJ raced to the puck as it dropped in behind the defence—and tallied an empty-net goal for Team Navy to ice the victory.

Seconds later, the buzzer sounded to officially end the game. Team Navy congregated at their goal and congratulated each other on their win.

Coach McIntosh announced his approval as the team returned to the dressing room. "Great effort, Navy! Way to battle back and show some grit and determination! We'll see you tomorrow."

CHAPTER VII

ADJUSTMENTS FOR TOMORROW

Following the skate, the coaching staff met inside the Revolution dressing room. Coach Fitzgerald and his two assistants wanted to evaluate the day's events and make any adjustments they felt were necessary before heading into Day Two of training camp.

"Well, I must say that it was a pretty entertaining game from up in the crowd," stated Coach Fitzgerald.

"Same from my bench," declared Coach McIntosh.

"And with mine," agreed Coach Horton, who had worked with Team Silver.

"Before I address what I saw," said Coach Fitzgerald, "was there anything worth noting from where you guys were standing?"

Coach Horton decided to take the lead. "Biggest story from Silver was Brad Martinsen's effort. The kid was dynamic and very positive on the bench. Really led our team in an all-around way and was a pleasure to have. Other bright spots were some older guys and their ability to play a strong two-way game. I'm thinking of Justin Norris and Steve Reinhart. Umm…" he paused to collect a few more thoughts. "Would like to see more from Jeremy Wright. Didn't think his line was great, but he showed signs of being able to do more. Just a few things off the top of my head."

"Great!" Coach Fitzgerald responded. "What do you want to do with Wright? Pop him up with Marty? Would be a similar style player to McDennis, and he is not an underager."

"That would be a good spot for him," Coach Horton agreed.

"We'll juggle things around a little then," Coach Fitzgerald said. "Any negatives?"

"Honestly, no," exclaimed Coach Horton. "Everyone was on their best behaviour."

"Good. How about Team Navy?" said Coach Fitzgerald as he turned to his other assistant.

"Much the same, I suppose," professed Coach McIntosh. "No issues. Really liked the Kelley line. Thought O'Connor was impressive. Anderson twins were quiet."

"Maybe we try the twins out on the other team tomorrow," Coach Fitzgerald announced. "What were your thoughts on Burrow?"

"Solid," replied Coach McIntosh. "Plays with a lot of poise and very impactful. I wasn't expecting that level of play from him."

"I want to see him play with DJ tomorrow," said Coach Fitzgerald enthusiastically. "He connected for one goal in the midst of a line change; maybe more is in store!"

"Give me Scott Parker on their right side," Coach McIntosh pleaded. "He showed some wheels out there today. Could be a good fit with those two."

"Okay," agreed Coach Fitzgerald. "How did you guys feel about the back end and in net? 'Cause I would like to flop Black and Freeman for the game tomorrow to give a different look on the top pairing for both sides."

"I like the sound of Sharp and Freeman together," said Coach McIntosh.

"And I get Black and Kraemer?" questioned Coach Horton rhetorically. "That suits me just fine!"

"As far as goaltending is concerned, I thought Riddle played well and McIntyre held a slight edge over the remaining goalies—mainly over Boushy," stated Coach Fitzgerald. "I would like to see all the goalies remain where they are, but have McIntyre and Boushy flip-flopped in the order."

"Start McIntyre and finish with Boushy?" said Coach McIntosh rhetorically. "Will do!"

"Well, guys," Coach Fitzgerald carried on, "I will write up the adjustments and get them to you this evening. Talk to you guys then!"

RING… RING… RING…

Marty reached over to his phone lethargically and answered the incoming call. "Hey."

"Ready to wear my beautiful Montreal jersey on Tuesday?" asked DJ with a laugh.

"Absolutely!" replied Marty sarcastically. "Tomorrow will be a different story, dude!"

DJ laughed and playfully replied, "No chance! Your only hope for victory is getting traded!"

"We'll see… we'll see," Marty responded boisterously. "So, how'd you feel after the game today? I thought your line was pretty dominant—tough to keep you guys from doing what you were wanting to do."

"Felt good… better as things went along! Thought we had some good chemistry. It was fun to play with those two guys—that's for sure. You were on fire out there, eh!?"

"All that training in the off-season, I guess," Marty chuckled. "Legs were feeling fresh! Felt like I was closing on plays twice as fast as I did last year."

"Yeah, we found that out a few times," exclaimed DJ. "Kip couldn't believe you were able to break up our one scoring chance."

Marty laughed. "Yeah, I remember!"

"Think there will be much change heading into tomorrow?"

"Hard to say," Marty replied thoughtfully. "Heard that a few guys were actually skating with other teams in the evening as well—talk about a long day!"

"Oh really? I didn't hear anyone saying that," DJ said with interest.

"Yeah. Matheson and the Andersons were going out with the Hawks, I guess," replied Marty. "Few others going elsewhere too."

"With the Hawks, eh!? They were pretty good last year."

"Finished top three in the standings," stated Marty. "Lost in the second round. Supposedly, they are going to be even stronger this year."

"Hmm…"

"They are pretty high on adding the twins, according to Matheson," Marty continued. "They have a few holes up front, but pretty loaded throughout their lineup. Matheson didn't think he had much of a chance."

"That's good… for the Andersons, at least," DJ said.

"Good for us, too," commented Marty. "Takes away two from the competition for the underage spots with the Revolution—if that's true."

"Yeah," DJ agreed. "You keep playing the way you did today and you don't have much to worry about, buddy!"

"Thanks, man! You too," said Marty enthusiastically.

"Anyway, I'll see you tomorrow morning. Have a good night!" said DJ.

"Good night!"

CHAPTER VIII

ΠAVY AND SILVER
GAME #2

The morning skates were energetic, much like Day One of training camp. All of the adjustments from the coaches were implemented and the players were able to practice with their linemates for the afternoon. DJ found himself on a line with big Brendan Burrow and speedy Scott Parker. The trio had a broad range of skill, as Burrow brought the physicality, Parker brought the flash, and DJ brought the finish. They worked well together in the line rushes conducted during Team Navy's time on the ice in the morning.

There were other changes in both squads' lineups, but the most notable difference was the absence of the Andersons. DJ wondered if his conversation with Marty proved to be accurate. He had a chance to converse with Marty after Team Silver's skate, so it didn't take long before he got his answer.

"So, what happened to the Andersons?" questioned DJ.

"Signed," Marty responded. "After last night's skate they committed to the Hawks!"

"Wow! That was fast!"

"Yeah. Matheson rode to the skate with them. Said they were far better with the Hawks than they were out here in the afternoon."

"Hmm, I guess they were just getting their legs going out here then," DJ wondered.

"Must've been."

The two friends wished each other the best of luck again as they split ways. The players on both teams began to focus on the upcoming game, knowing this was their last chance to influence the Revolution's staff this weekend.

Team Navy and Team Silver hit the ice flying as they prepared for the opening faceoff. DJ and his newly formed line made their way to their bench as the referees signalled the start of the game. The line made up of Kip Kelley, O'Connor and Dozer lined up at centre to faceoff against Marty, Gage and Wright.

Kip and Marty renewed their acquaintance as they took the opening draw—with Kip earning a win. Freeman chipped the puck off the boards and in behind Team Silver's defence. Dozer applied some pressure on Black—his teammate from a day ago. Black was able to control the puck and send a pass across to his partner. Kraemer took a glance up the ice and sent a firm pass to Marty circling just inside the blueline.

Marty brought the puck up toward the redline before being forced into making a decision by his opposing centreman. Kip closed in and took away Marty's space, which left him with no option but to dump the puck in deep. Following the release of the puck, Kip finished his check on the smaller-sized defenceman.

"Going to have to earn it today," Kip shouted as Marty lay on the ice.

Marty shook off the hit—and the comment—and returned to his feet. In Team Navy's zone, Freeman gained control of the puck and set up behind his own net. He began to move out as Wright pressed in on his left side. Freeman sent a cross-ice pass to a streaking O'Connor—allowing the left-winger to maintain his speed as he entered the neutral zone. O'Connor chipped the puck by Kraemer and regained possession as he moved into a 1-on-1 with Black.

O'Connor drove the defender back into his own zone, however, Black sustained his strong position on the winger. O'Connor attempted to slide the puck through Black's feet and jump around him to the middle of the ice, but the sturdy defenceman stood up and knocked O'Connor off his feet with a clean check.

The intensity of the second intersquad game was evident as the two teams continued to battle it out during the first period. DJ's line was able to generate some offensive zone time, but they were unable to break down Team Silver and produce any quality scoring chances.

"Really tight game today, guys," announced Coach McIntosh from the Navy bench. "Need to dig deep to get into those scoring areas."

A few shifts later, Team Silver's line consisting of Drake Murray, Steve Reinhart and Mike McDennis forced the puck in deep and were applying some steady pressure. The trio were able to create a turnover as the defence moved the puck up the wall to the wing. McDennis, who created the turnover, cycled the puck back in to Reinhart behind the goal. Reinhart picked up the puck and shielded it from the oncoming defender. He worked the puck back toward McDennis, who came down low to help his centre.

McDennis used his strength to work his way out of the corner and was able to fire a shot on the goaltender, Spencer McIntyre. McIntyre dropped into a butterfly and deflected the puck away.

The puck bounced over to the boards, and Kraemer moved in promptly to keep the pressure alive. Kraemer picked up the puck and threw another hard, low shot at the goal. McDennis was able to get his stick on the shot as it headed in on McIntyre. The puck changed direction and found a hole just over McIntyre's pad—giving Team Silver a 1–0 lead.

The battle on the ice continued, but neither side was able to change the scoreboard before the end of the first period. The two teams left the ice as the intermission began, with players on both sides in desperate need of the break.

"Keep up the good work," Coach McIntosh stated as he popped his head into the room during the break. "We'll get the results we're aiming for if we keep this work ethic."

DJ and the rest of Team Navy were quietly anticipating the next period, and before long they were summoned back to the ice.

Kip Kelley, who found himself centring two lines due to the twins' absence, made his way back to the faceoff circle. His opponent, once again, was Brad Martinsen. The two clashed again for the faceoff—with Marty using a quick shift in body position to kick the puck back to Kraemer. Marty's move was received with a cross-check to the back from Kip. Marty felt an immediate jolt of pain and let out a sharp yelp. The referee witnessed the play up close, and didn't hesitate to raise his arm to signal a penalty call.

"Are you kidding me?" screamed Kip as he saw the ref's reaction. Kraemer had already sent the puck deep, leading to a whistle when Sam Nectle scooped up the puck. "Have to be tougher than that, kid!" Kip yelled in Marty's direction as he skated to the penalty box.

Marty shrugged off Kip one more time as he moved in for the offensive zone faceoff to start the power play. The duo of DJ and Burrow were tapped on the shoulders and sent out to kill the start of the penalty.

On the upcoming draw, Burrow used his strength to muscle the puck back to Freeman. Freeman instantly fired the puck hard off the glass to relieve the initial pressure from the power play. Kraemer had already backtracked out of the zone and went back to gather up the puck in his own zone. Team Silver swung back and began to move up the ice together. Kraemer held onto control as he worked his way up the ice. DJ held his position in the middle and forced the puck carrier to make a decision with it—Kraemer dropped the puck to Marty who had gathered up some speed in behind him.

Marty flew up and beyond DJ, where he met Burrow. With a quick snap, Marty sent out a pass to Harrison Gage, who then proceeded to enter the offensive zone. Gage rimmed the puck hard around the boards as Freeman took away his ice—Wright picked it up in the far corner. Wright saw Marty move in toward the half wall and dished it up to the crafty centre. Marty stopped on a dime, and the power play shifted into an umbrella formation. Working it back and forth with Kraemer a few times, Marty continued to examine his options in the zone.

DJ was positioned on that side and took away as much time and space as he could, but the two offensive-minded skaters were a challenge. The puck moved up to Kraemer again, and the defenceman looked to send a shot through—causing DJ to commit on the play. Kraemer faked the shot, and he returned the puck back to Marty who now had an open avenue into the slot. Marty didn't waste any time and skated in with the puck across the top of the circle.

Team Navy penalty killers closed in on him to take away a clean opportunity, but Marty anticipated this and kept his radar up. Sharp was one of the players to step up, leaving Wright wide open down on the goal line beside the net. Marty sent a quick pass through Sharp, perfectly aimed for Wright's stick. Taking control, Wright took a few hard strides toward the top of the crease and jammed the puck along the ice.

Sam Nectle had read the play and met the shot with his right pad, but the puck bounced out quickly and was met by the stick of Harrison Gage, who had filtered in from the weak side. Gage one-touched the puck back in toward the gaping net for the goal.

For the second straight day, Team Silver had gained a 2–0 lead. The five on the ice all came together to celebrate the goal; Team Navy tapped Sam Nectle on the pads and returned to their bench with lowered heads.

"Sorry, guys," announced Kip as he returned to the bench after the goal. "Bad play on my part." He made sure to tap gloves with the players that attempted to kill the penalty—acknowledging their effort following his mistake.

"Have to get that back for us now, Kipper," stated Freeman as he came up to him.

Team Navy didn't have much time to hang their heads in sorrow, as Team Silver continued the pressure following their second goal. Their line featuring JJ Turcotte followed up the power play crew and brought the puck right back in to test Team Navy in their defensive zone.

Turcotte picked up the puck low and skated the puck behind Nectle in net. Turcotte had his head up, looking for one of his wingers looming behind their coverage. No lanes opened up, so he continued into the corner and up the half wall. Stewart Cooke—a smart veteran player coming to the team with Junior B experience—closed in on the offensive-minded centre and forced Turcotte to shoot the puck back below the goal. Matt Manson was first to the loose puck. As Manson gained control of the puck, the physical Andrew Boersman drilled him hard into the boards. Manson crumbled to the ice and Boersman took control of the puck. Unfortunately for Boersman, the ref deemed that the contact was in the danger zone and blew the play dead.

Boersman was furious with the call, but he went quietly to the box to serve two minutes for boarding. Once again, Team Silver would bring their power play out onto the ice and would try to take a three-goal lead. Turcotte remained on the ice and was joined by Marty's line and Kraemer. They were met by the combination of Cooke, Zalapski, Gillies and Redman.

Marty won the faceoff to begin the power play with offensive possession. Turcotte was the recipient of the win and he fed the puck to Kraemer with a quick pass. Kraemer wasted no time in his shot attempt, but the hard wrister was met by the leather glove of Sam Nectle—the play was brought to a stoppage right away.

The players lined up again, with Marty winning another back to Turcotte. Turcotte one-touched the puck again to Kraemer, however, this time Kraemer pump-faked a shot and settled down into possession with the puck as his teammates moved into position. He sent the puck back to Turcotte, who then played the puck to Marty. Marty had Cooke covering his lane to the net, but he decided to skate with the puck and engage the defender. Cooke had to respect Marty's mobility, so he backed in and tried to take away Marty's lane as he entered into the middle of the ice.

Turcotte filtered in behind Marty and received a drop pass from him as he entered the open ice that was created for him. Marty continued across the ice and Kraemer filled the middle—Zalapski read the play well on the defensive side and called for a switch with Cooke. Turcotte's space was promptly taken away by the smaller defender and he was left with fewer options because of it.

"Down low!" yelled Harrison Gage as he broke off from his screen in front of the net.

Turcotte flung the puck down below the goal line to Gage. Gage opened up with possession and saw Marty sneak down on the weak side. With no direct passing lane available, Gage banked a pass along the end boards to his centre. Marty picked the puck up effortlessly and watched as the defenders shifted across the ice. As well as watching how the coverage played out, Marty kept a keen eye on Jeremy Wright out front of the net. As big Donald Redman released from Wright out front to take away any potential jam play from Marty, the right winger was left momentarily unattended and the creative centre sent a beautiful pass between Redman's outstretched stick and body. Wright met the pass with forward motion from his stick, sending a one-timer past Nectle's glove—taking the score to 3–0, Silver. Again, Team Navy watched as their opponents celebrated the power-play goal.

"Discipline!" preached Coach McIntosh from behind the players on the bench. "Kelley, O'Connor and Stevenson—you're up!"

The three forwards hopped the boards and went directly to their respective positions at centre ice. Reinhart, Murray and McDennis lined up against them. Kip bared down on the draw and pulled it back to his defence. Redman gained control and moved the puck up to Dozer; the big winger gained entry into the offensive zone. Dozer wound up for a slapshot from the perimeter and sent a rocket in on goal, but it was turned away into the corner by Matt Murphy. O'Connor was able to streak in on the left side, pick up the puck off the ricochet and continue skating in below the net.

"Middle! Middle!" screeched Kip as he broke free from Reinhart in the slot.

O'Connor heard his linemate and sent a no-look pass out front. Kip cradled the puck and found himself all alone with Murphy. The goaltender challenged the opposing centreman, but Kip was patient with the puck, faked a quick release and deked Murphy on his forehand. He slid the puck into the goal, decreasing the lead to 3–1 with 16:30 left in the second period. The goal lifted Team Navy's spirits and they built off the momentum it generated. They continued to swarm 5-on-5 and outshot Team Silver mightily as the period wore on.

DJ's line hit the ice with just under a minute to go and they went on the attack right away. Brendan Burrow had created a neutral zone turnover and sprung DJ on a 2-on-2 rush with Parker. Victor Sharp had the presence of mind to jump up in the play and create an odd-man rush.

"With you, DJ!" hollered the defenceman in order to make his existence known.

Scott Parker drove hard to the net and opened up the high slot for Sharp to skate into. Drawing the primary defender down deeper into the zone with him, DJ floated a puck into the middle where Sharp met the puck with a booming slap shot. The shot sizzled over Murphy's right shoulder, but drilled the crossbar and flew out of play. Team Navy had been within a hair of bringing the game back to a one-goal difference.

Burrow lined up for the offensive zone faceoff with JJ Turcotte. DJ positioned himself on the boards and anticipated the puck drop, moving in to support Burrow as he won the puck and sent it behind himself. His jump on the defenders gave him time to scoop up the loose puck and fire a quick, low shot through the screen of the oncoming opponents. The shot caught Murphy by surprise and he was late to react, allowing it to beat him through the five-hole—Team Silver's lead was now down to only one. The remaining seconds of the period ticked off the clock with little to nothing amounting from them.

Kip Kelley skated toward DJ as they left the ice. "Nice shot, DJ," he complimented the winger as he gave him a pat on the helmet. "That was a great release!"

"Thanks Kipper!" replied DJ. "Way to get to the open area on your goal, too."

"Let's get another comeback win here today," added Kip. "Show them who's the boss!"

CHAPTER IX

PERIOD THREE

Up in the stands, Coach Fitzgerald, GM Flaherty and Assistant GM Chambers discussed the game heavily. Some of the player movement that Coach Fitzgerald implemented had paid dividends and they were able to see how the players reacted in new situations on Day Two.

"I'm really noticing Jeremy Wright out there today," exclaimed Assistant GM Chambers. "He's taking advantage of playing with Martinsen and Gage—that's good to see!"

"Good to see the response from several guys," agreed Coach Fitzgerald.

"I've got some good news coming our way on Wednesday," announced GM Flaherty. "Trent Rosenberg!"

"Really?" said Assistant GM Chambers keenly.

"Who's this?" asked an interested Coach Fitzgerald.

"Rosenberg played up in Ottawa with Kip Kelley," explained GM Flaherty. "I had called up to see how things were going with him, as Kip had mentioned that he may not want to stay. Played in the middle six up there last year, posted some decent stats... right winger." He looked at his assistant. "Have those numbers, Doug?"

"I'll have a quick look here," he answered as he pulled out his phone and scrolled through a few screens.

"What's his story? Why's he not sticking around?" pondered Coach Fitzgerald.

"Homesick," answered GM Flaherty. "Grew up not too far from here—Kitchener area."

"Got it," interrupted Assistant GM Chambers. "Played 62 games—had 15 goals and 23 assists."

"How old?" Coach Fitzgerald wondered.

"He'll be 18 this year," Assistant GM Chambers responded.

"Thirty-eight points in 62 games, in Major Junior as a 17-year-old..." detailed Coach Fitzgerald out loud. "Good size?"

"Has him listed at 6'1", 195 lbs," stated Assistant GM Chambers. "Last year's stats, so probably accurate enough for this season as well."

"Must have an agent working with him, eh, Bob?" inquired Coach Fitzgerald.

"Just his dad, actually," replied GM Flaherty.

"Hmm... pro scouts interested in him?" asked Coach Fitzgerald.

"Mild at best, I assume," said Assistant GM Chambers. "Doesn't have a ranking."

"Well," began Coach Fitzgerald, "let's hope we've got a steal here, gentlemen!"

The teams had returned to the ice and continued playing at the same intensity displayed during the first two periods. Team Silver seemed to collect themselves after relinquishing a commanding lead, and they were set to try and build on the one-goal lead they currently maintained.

Marty continued to buzz around the offensive zone and create havoc for Team Navy defensively. His poise with the puck and awareness of his teammates made each play a potential scoring threat. Just as soon as Marty's line left the ice, Team Navy returned the favour with Kip Kelley and company.

The back-and-forth action resulted in plenty of shots for the two new goaltenders, which allowed them to get into rhythm in their respective nets. Edward Boushy looked strong in net for Team Navy, and his counterpart, David Powers, knew that he would be under attack as his opposition looked for the tying goal. However, time continued to move forward and the halfway mark of the period approached.

"Come on, Navy!" Coach McIntosh voiced energetically. "Take it to another level here! Foot down on the gas!"

The players heard the plea from their coach and tried to find it within themselves to find a new gear.

"Let's pick it up here, guys!" said DJ to Burrow and Parker positively. "We've got this!"

The trio watched attentively from the bench as they awaited their next shift. Kip Kelley's line was able to force the puck deep and get a whistle—Coach McIntosh sent DJ's line out for the offensive zone faceoff.

They lined up in the same format as they had for DJ's second period goal, and the plan was to repeat their success. However, Burrow lost the draw to Steve Reinhart and Wallace Black gained control of the puck in the defensive zone. Parker quickly jumped in from the slot and took away the defenceman's ability to skate with the puck—Black was forced to rim it around to the weak side to prevent a turnover.

McDennis raced over to try to chip the puck out of the zone, but Victor Sharp used his fleet feet to beat McDennis to the puck. Sharp poked the puck back down into the corner. DJ had come off the wall on the faceoff and entered into a supportive position immediately as the play had unfolded, allowing him to be first into the corner to retrieve the puck.

DJ knew he didn't have much time to maneuver as Curtis Kraemer closed in on him, so he protected the puck and bought time for his linemates to come in and pick it up. Kraemer pinned DJ along the boards and dug for the puck, but DJ successfully managed to keep the defender from stripping him of possession.

Burrow slid in to help, pulled the puck out and skated behind the net. He took a look out front, but he didn't risk forcing a play to a well-covered Scott Parker. Instead, he banked a pass out toward the blueline. Freeman pulled the puck off the wall and opened up toward the middle of the ice.

With his head up, Freeman noted DJ sliding in off the weak side of the net as he freed up from coverage, while Kraemer chased Burrow behind the goal. Freeman snapped the puck off to the left side of Matt Murphy—directly at DJ's stick. DJ made no mistake in his redirection of the puck, tying the game 3–3.

The players on the bench erupted with admiration for their teammate's effort toward the tying goal. DJ skated toward Freeman, pointing at the defencemen the entire way to acknowledge the superb play.

"Great pass, Dally!" expressed DJ as he high-fived the veteran rearguard.

"You got to the area and put it in the net," replied Freeman. "All I had to do was get it there."

The teams lined up for the next faceoff at centre ice. The players knew the last half of the period would be a dog fight. Kip Kelley once again found himself battling Brad Martinsen as the two centres came together. Marty swung for the dropped puck and connected on his backhand, pulling the puck back. Team Silver pushed up the ice and pressured Team Navy as they tried to respond to the three unanswered goals that had brought the game back to square one.

Harrison Gage worked the puck low with Jeremy Wright, as the two looked to break down some in-zone coverage and gain a scoring opportunity. Marty entered the scene and gave the wingers an outlet up the wall. Marty gathered the puck and drew in the defender. As he moved out toward the blueline, he chipped the puck back down to Gage and then curled hard to the slot seeking a return pass. Gage saw his chance and returned the pass.

Marty received the pass, then… *SMASH*!

Kip delivered a massive hit on his adversary and created a turnover for his team.

Andrew Boersman scooped up the loose puck and passed it quickly to Chase Livermore who broke through the middle of the ice. Livermore flew up the ice on the attack with Levi Provolie. Marty remained down on the ice.

TWEET…

The referee's whistle sounded and the gathering crowd waved for the trainer to attend to the fallen skater. Dr. Andrews made his way into the huddle and knelt beside Marty.

"Brad?" said Dr. Andrews as he checked whether the player was conscious.

"Yeah?" responded a confused Brad Martinsen. "What happened?"

"You took a big hit. Do you know where you are?"

"Uhh… at the Revolution training camp," said Marty unsteadily.

"Are you having any pain in your neck?"

"Bit sore… I suppose."

"Can you wiggle your fingertips… toes?"

"Yes."

"Okay, good. How about your head? Headache or dizzy?"

"Bit dizzy. Feeling some pressure in my head."

"Take your time, but I think we can help you up and get you off to have a further examination in the trainer's room," said Dr. Andrews. "Then we'll get you up to the hospital, alright?"

"Sounds good," replied Marty as he began to push himself up. DJ and Kip—of all people—moved in to help support Marty as he got to his feet. Once he was up, the two players helped usher him toward the gate.

"Hey, buddy," started Kip. "Sorry about the hit. I wasn't meaning for this to happen—I was just trying to make a check…"

"Okay," answered Marty, still confused and unaware of what had actually transpired on the play leading up to him being on the ice. When they reached the gate, DJ and Kip were relieved of their duties as the Revolution staff members took over. The two skaters returned to their bench.

"It wasn't bad, right DJ?" asked Kip as he looked for confirmation.

"I didn't really see it, to be honest," said DJ. In reality, DJ had witnessed the hit and thought that it seemed a bit deliberate considering the growing rivalry between the two centres. "We all know hitting is a part of the game, and Marty does too. He won't take it personally."

"Yeah, injuries happen, unfortunately," responded Kip, somewhat insensitively.

"Yeah," agreed DJ reluctantly. DJ wasn't very impressed with Kip's actions and remarks. He felt awful for his best friend. Marty had been playing some of his best hockey and would definitely have a setback if he were dealing with a concussion or some other type of head or neck trauma. Fortunately for Marty, Dr. Andrews was an ultimate professional and Marty would be taken care of properly.

DJ, however, had to put aside his thoughts about Marty's wellbeing for the remaining portion of the game. The play resumed and DJ watched from the bench, still somewhat in disbelief of what had just occurred. But as play progressed, his focus returned to the ice completely. DJ was due up as the play continued down toward Team Silver's zone—Dominic O'Connor raised his stick and skated to the bench. DJ saw that O'Connor was signalling a line change, so he got to his feet and hopped over the boards.

By now, Team Silver had transitioned into a breakout and were skating back toward DJ and his two defencemen. The three of them lined up across the redline and tried to bunch up the area as much as they could. JJ Turcotte led the attack and as he ran out of skating room, he sent a pass to Anson Brown. Brown took control of the puck, but a quick stick check from Donald Redman sent the puck back in the opposite direction—trapping four skaters up ice.

Dozer was hustling back and profited from Redman's strong stick. He scooped up the puck and curled back into the offensive zone. DJ jumped up into the play and turned it into a 2-on-1 attack on defenceman Eric Matheson. Dozer was aware of DJ and sent a quick, hard pass to him as he crossed the blueline.

DJ cradled the strong pass effortlessly and moved in on his strong side. Matheson knew he had to make a bold move in order to break up the attack, so he dropped down to the ice to take away as much of the shooting and passing lane as possible. DJ was a step ahead of the defender though, and he hit the brakes and toe dragged the puck up and around Matheson before sending a tap-in pass to Stevenson—bringing the score to 4–3 for Team Navy.

"Whoo!" screeched Dozer as he stopped and picked DJ up off his skates in celebration. "What a play, brother!" DJ could only laugh and smile at the dramatic response from his friend. The two were joined by the rest of the skaters on the ice.

"Great stick, Red," complimented DJ. "Way to use that massive reach!"

Team Navy continued to press in the remaining minutes of the game, but they were unable to create a two-goal spread. This left the game open for some last minute theatrics, as Team Silver returned JJ Turcotte's line to the ice. The line was able to get the puck in and force Edward Boushy to freeze it—resulting in an offensive zone faceoff for Team Silver.

DJ, Burrow and Parker were sent over the boards to take on the responsibility of defending the lead inside the last minute of play; they were accompanied by Freeman and Redman. Team Silver left Turcotte on the ice, and added Gage, Wright, McDennis, Kraemer and Black to push for the tie.

Turcotte and Burrow moved in for the draw—Burrow won it back to the corner. Team Silver applied immediate pressure as Freeman gained control, compelling him to fire a hard shot around the boards. Black met the clearing attempt at the blueline and kept the play alive. Black took a few strides down into the zone and sent a knee-high wrister toward the net—Redman blocked the shot and the puck deflected back into the corner.

"Protect the house!" hollered Coach McIntosh from the bench, as he urged Team Navy to remain strong in front of their net.

Harrison Gage was on the loose puck in a hurry and used the open lane up the boards to return the puck back to Black. Black's lane to the net was not available on round two, so he dished the puck to his partner. As the offensively-gifted Kraemer garnered possession, DJ stepped up and tried to poke the puck outside the zone. However, Kraemer swiftly moved the puck through an open seam back down low to Gage.

Gage was given some space to step out from the corner and rifled a low shot into the goalie's pads—hoping to catch Boushy off guard and either score or create a rebound opportunity. He was correct in his assessment of the situation. Boushy kicked the puck back into the slot area, right to where McDennis lurked. McDennis connected the oncoming puck with a hard snap shot—forcing Boushy to make an incredibly athletic glove save. Boushy held onto the puck for another whistle.

DJ circled in to his goaltender. "Unbelievable save, Eddy!" He tapped his goaltender on the pad and then returned to his position to the left of the upcoming faceoff.

Burrow won the draw once again, but Gage shot through the gap and retrieved the puck in behind the centreman. Gage fired a shot along the ice into Boushy's feet, trying to create some chaos in the dying seconds of the game.

Boushy kicked the puck out and into the slot once more and he scrambled to track the rebound. An ensuing puck battle occurred as several members from both sides fought for possession in the slot. McDennis tried to dig the puck free, but Freeman held steady and knocked the winger off balance. Scott Parker finally got his stick on the loose puck and lobbed a shot out toward the neutral zone. It was high, but not high enough, as the 6′5″ Wallace Black was able to jump and reach it with his glove. Black threw the puck down to the ice—knowing time was running out—and fired a bullet from just inside the blueline.

TING…

The puck nearly blew a hole in the post as it connected, but the shot fired off to the boards. The siren sounded before anyone could get to the puck. The final score was 4–3 for Team Navy.

CHAPTER X

MEETING WITH THE REVOLUTION STAFF

The Team Navy players filtered into the dressing room following the game and were very excited after the second straight come-from-behind victory.

Coach McIntosh congratulated the squad on the hard work they had displayed and their relentless effort to come back from the 3–0 deficit. He also relayed the message that all the players needed to come down to the Revolution dressing room to meet with the staff. The endorphins were still running high, but reality settled in as each player knew that their individual status was still in the evaluation process.

"Hey, guys!" Kip Kelley shouted as he stood up to address his teammates. "Good job out there this weekend. We all worked together to get the job done, and that shouldn't go unnoticed." The team cheered in agreement. DJ knew Kip had some great qualities as a leader, but he was still uneasy over what had happened to Marty. He truly hoped that he would get to know Kip in a better way and put to rest any doubt over whether the hit on Marty was deliberately meant to injure his best friend.

DJ got undressed rather quickly. He knew that showing some urgency toward meeting with the Revolution staff would likely be seen as a positive measure on his part. He then hopped into the shower and cleaned up before heading down the hallway to the team dressing room. The door to the dressing room was propped open and he entered the room. Surprisingly, he was one of the first players down, so he grabbed a seat in one of the stalls as he waited his turn to meet with the staff. The players scheduled before him entered the office and were dismissed within a few minutes, as the staff didn't want to hold up the process of dealing with 40-plus individuals any longer than was needed.

DJ sat patiently and was finally waved into the office by GM Flaherty. "Come on in, DJ!" Getting up from his seat, DJ felt confident and believed the upcoming meeting would go well.

"Well, DJ," began GM Flaherty, "from my standpoint, you did everything that was expected from you. I was very pleased with your effort this weekend." He looked over to the head coach. "Coach Fitzgerald?"

"Yes," he declared. "I was very impressed. You looked very poised on the ice and displayed great physical and mental awareness. Everyone in here believes in your talent."

DJ felt slightly embarrassed as he received the praise. "Thank you very much."

"Our two underage cards will be very important this season," Coach Fitzgerald continued. "The two players that are signed are going to play significant roles on this team— this season and going forward. You appear to be very worthy of one of those cards… but the competition is strong. I want to watch how you young guys compete in the upcoming tournament before going forward with the signing process. The Andersons—if you weren't already aware—signed with the Hawks, but I am not going to be forced into making a decision before being fully aware of what talent I have in front of me, understand?"

"Yes, completely," agreed DJ as he listened closely to the coach.

"This team—if all goes according to plan—will be competitive from the onset, and players like yourself could use this as an opportunity to showcase yourself," Coach Fitzgerald said. "I don't want you to feel discouraged about not signing after such a strong showing. Stay strong and continue to prove what you can do on the ice. We'll see you Wednesday night, DJ."

"Yes, thank you Coach," replied DJ. He stood up from his seat and shook hands with Coach Fitzgerald.

"See you later, DJ," said GM Flaherty as he opened the door up for DJ to leave.

DJ left the Revolution dressing room and returned to pick up his bag from Dressing Room Four. On his way back, he met Joel Stevenson in the hallway.

"How did that go?" asked Dozer.

"Fine… I suppose," DJ responded half-heartedly. "They said they liked what they saw and want me to keep working hard. They want to see how all the underagers do in the tournament before making any final decisions."

"Hmm… that's surprising they didn't lock you up right away," said a puzzled Dozer. "You were dominating out there—both skates!"

"Oh well. I understand what Coach was saying. I'm not taking it personal. I just have to keep on going forward!"

"Yeah," sighed Dozer.

"All the best in your meeting, eh!" expressed DJ. He shook hands with his friend.

"Thanks. See you later," Dozer said as he turned and headed in the opposite direction.

The meetings in the Revolution's office continued over the next hour or so. They were forced to make a few tough decisions on whether or not to advance certain individuals. Wednesday night's practice would be conducted in one session, so the numbers needed to be chopped down marginally. The consensus was that they would have 18 forwards, 10 defencemen and 3 goaltenders heading into Wednesday. Additionally, the majority—if not all—would be included in the Labour Day Classic Junior A Hockey Tournament.

There would be five other teams competing in the exhibition tournament, allowing each team the opportunity to evaluate their talent more extensively. The bonus— especially for a team heading into their first season—was that the teams would be able to scout some of the competition and keep an eye on any players that could become available when cuts were made.

The Revolution staff compiled their lineup of players that would be invited back on Wednesday. They printed a copy of the list.

<u>Wednesday Night Line Combinations</u>

<u>Navy Jerseys</u>
Dominic O'Connor – Kip Kelley – Trent Rosenberg

Mike McDennis [U] – Stewart Cooke – James Northgate
Justin Norris – Steve Reinhart – Scott Parker

Victor Sharp [U] – Dallas Freeman
Eric Matheson [U] – Donald Redman
Matthew MacKenzie

Carter Riddle

<u>Silver Jerseys</u>
Harrison Gage – JJ Turcotte – Jeremy Wright
DJ Roberts [U] – Brendan Burrow [U] – Joel Stevenson
Anson Brown – Kole Kelley – Matt Manson

Wallace Black – Curtis Kraemer
Andrew Boersman – Cody Ryerson
Mike Killington

Edward Boushy
Spencer McIntyre

*[U] Indicates Underage Skater

Several underage players were not making the transition from the weekend, leaving six in competition for the two spots. Wednesday night's lineup would consist of five underage skaters. Brad Martinsen was still considered a prime candidate for one of the cards, however, the staff would have to make a decision regarding the injured skater when the severity of his injury was known.

The Revolution management and coaching staff also had to decide who they would offer cards to following the initial weekend of camp. They were well aware of the nature of sports and how the current time of year could be a now-or-never opportunity to sign certain individuals. With many camps happening across the province—at all different levels—they wanted to sign the individuals they felt showcased themselves as "must sign" players.

When the topic came up, the names of Dominic O'Connor, Curtis Kraemer, Jeremy Wright, Stewart Cooke, Donald Redman and Joel Stevenson all came up as potential signees. The discussion had to be brief, as the staff only had a few minutes prior to or between speaking to all the players that had attended the camp that weekend.

"In my mind, I think all of these skaters need to be offered a card tonight," stated GM Flaherty. "They represented themselves strongly on the ice and will help fill out our lineup. I don't think we can afford to let them sit in limbo and potentially find their way elsewhere."

"I'm good with this," agreed Assistant GM Chambers. "We knew coming in that we would be forced to act quick on available talent... and these guys proved themselves worthy in my book."

"It would be nice to stretch it out," stated Coach Fitzgerald. "But... I don't want to risk losing players that can play—and each of them proved they can."

"All good with signing them then?" GM Flaherty asked for a final approval. The staff approved unanimously.

"Is that as far as we go?" questioned Assistant Coach McIntosh. "Thinking of guys like Parker, Boersman, Ryerson..."

"If all the aforementioned sign, we sit at eight forwards, four defencemen and a goalie," declared GM Flaherty. "Still holds for some competition as we progress."

"Plus Trent Rosenberg," added Assistant GM Chambers.

"Right," agreed GM Flaherty. "That essentially is nine forwards."

"Okay," concurred Assistant Coach McIntosh.

"And we are always looking at bringing in talent from outside the organization," announced GM Flaherty firmly. "We will always be trying to find a way to make the Revolution a better team!"

The staff concluded their discussion and carried on with the player meetings. They were very positive and supportive of all the players they parted ways with, and they made sure to let them know the team would keep an eye on them wherever they wound up. Certain players, such as goaltenders Sam Nectle and Matt Murphy, were encouraged to go play somewhere where they would be given a chance to play as an underage eligible player. As goaltenders, they needed playing time. Coach Fitzgerald suggested that another year in AAA might be the best option for both of them.

In Sam Nectle's case, the team made sure to let him know that he was welcome to attend practice over the course of the season, as he was a local talent. They also notified him of the potential need to use him as an affiliate over the upcoming year. Sam, while obviously disheartened from being let go, knew that this would be a good chance to connect with the team and open the door for him down the line.

The signing process for the team went well, as all six players that were offered a card agreed to sign. This was, as management had discussed, a large step in taking away the uncertainty of the team's roster going forward. Now with the 12 skaters signed and Carter Riddle between the pipes, the core of the team looked very healthy. The next opportunity to fill the remaining openings would be based on the upcoming tournament play—and players like DJ relished the chance to make a statement.

CHAPTER XI

MAKING NEWS

The sun was already shining through the window as DJ woke up Monday. DJ ensured that he would take full advantage of the break by getting as much sleep as possible following the rigorous weekend on the ice. He got up and glanced at his clock—it was already 10:00 am. The demanding effort needed over the four ice sessions had taken a toll on his body, but all in all, DJ felt refreshed and ready to take on the day. Racing down the stairs and into the kitchen, he saw the newspaper on the kitchen table. DJ sat down and began to read an article from the sports section of *The Journal*.

Revolution Hit the Ice
by Dean Moore

The Junior A Revolution took to the ice for their first training camp in team history. The long-awaited camp opened with a bang as Team Navy and Team Silver faced off in a two-day series during the evaluation period.

When asked about his first impression of the talent on the ice, Head Coach Steve Fitzgerald said he was "excited" and "very pleased with the how the players on both squads played." He also relayed that, "We [the Revolution] are pleased to announce the signing of six more skaters following the game." The players he referred to were forwards Dominic O'Connor, Jeremy Wright, Stewart Cooke and Joel Stevenson, as well as defencemen Curtis Kraemer and Donald Redman.

Hometown product, Joel Stevenson, was very honoured to be included on that list. "I think as a local player, you really appreciate the opportunity to play for your hometown team. To be linked with the other players already signed is a big accomplishment." Stevenson showed why he was part of the group with his play on the ice. The 6'3" forward displayed the physical prowess expected and also chipped in with a goal and two assists over the weekend.

Other top performers included hometown players such as Kip Kelley, Brad Martinsen and DJ Roberts. Kelley was brought back from his tenure with Ottawa and is expected to lead the upstart team. "Kip brings valued experience and leadership," stated GM Bob Flaherty. "He really understands the game and plays at an elite level." Kelley registered a goal and an assist on the opening day, and followed that up with another goal on Sunday.

The duo of Martinsen and Roberts have made the headlines before, but the story of these two usually comes from the same side of the battle. Over the two games this weekend, they went head-to-head. The two players are considered "underage" players and are in competition for the only two cards available for their classification. GM Flaherty mentioned, "It is very important to see these two players as individuals. We know what they can accomplish together." Indeed, the two young players were dynamic in previous years together, most recently delivering an Ontario Championship.

Martinsen looked very strong over the two-day event—scoring a goal and adding three assists. Unfortunately for the small centre, he endured an injury in the third period on Sunday and was forced to leave the ice. "You never want to see that happen," said Coach Fitzgerald following the game. "A young talent trying to make a case for himself—it's especially difficult in his situation." The status for Martinsen's return is still unknown, but the team is very hopeful they will see him soon. "We hope he can return to the ice shortly. I know what he has put in to be ready for this camp," said GM Flaherty.

Maybe the biggest surprise of the weekend, when all was said and done, was DJ Roberts remaining unsigned. The winger was dynamic and contributed four goals and two assists, but Coach Fitzgerald said he was very open about what he wanted. "I told him [DJ] that I wanted to see the compete level remain high, and even taken to another level. We want those underage cards filled with players that will play significant roles this season and I told him that. The upcoming tournament is big for these players—we have six skaters vying for two spots."

While Roberts clearly demonstrated his ability this weekend, the cast of Brendan Burrow, Mike McDennis, Victor Sharp and Eric Matheson all will join Roberts in competing for an underage card during the Labour Day Classic Tournament. The Revolution are set to begin on Friday night as they faceoff with last year's third overall seed—The Hawks.

DJ had mixed feelings as he closed the paper. On the positive side, he was extremely happy with his play and the kind words said about him. He was also very excited to play in the upcoming tournament, as he cherished the difficulties found in competition and loved having to raise his personal compete level. On the other side of the matter was the ordeal revolving around Marty and his injury. Ever since the two began to focus on training to become members of the Revolution, their goal had been to make it together and continue their legacy as linemates. Now DJ seriously questioned whether they would have that opportunity.

He decided that he should take this time to check in with his best friend and inquire about the extent of the injury. DJ dialed the number on his phone, but it went straight through to Marty's voicemail. DJ hung up and decided to write a text to his friend instead.

DJ wrote, *"Hey, just tried calling. Wanted to see how you were doing?"*

While he waited for a response, DJ carried on with his morning activities. He put together a huge breakfast—a three-egg omelette with cheese, onion and mushroom, and a side of toast—and went out to the living room to tune into the morning highlights.

DING…

He had received a message, so without hesitation, he put all else on hold.

"Hey DJ. Pretty rough night for me. They wanted to run some tests at the hospital and was up there for a few hours," replied Marty.

DJ wrote back, *"Man… doesn't sound like fun. What's it looking like?"*

Marty responded quickly. *"Concussion and whiplash… out indefinitely at this point."*

While DJ understood the seriousness of what Marty was dealing with, it was still a tough thing to comprehend. *"I feel terrible for you buddy… this sucks!"*

"Thanks for thinking of me, man. I really appreciate it! Don't worry, I'll be back before you know it!"

DJ knew his friend was very resilient and highly motivated, but he also knew the timetable for his return would keep him out of the lineup for at least the first few weeks of the season. He wondered what the Revolution staff would do—would they hold off on signing a card because of it, or would they take a different approach with who they sign? Of course, DJ fully anticipated signing a card, but his heart desired the second spot for his best friend.

"Have you talked to the team yet?" DJ questioned.

"Dr. Andrews knows and will pass along the message. I will likely meet with them Wednesday night during practice."

"Have any idea how they will take it? What did Dr. Andrews say?"

"No idea... not really trying to think about that part of it to be honest. Dr. Andrews said he was optimistic about things..."

"Okay buddy... well I'll see you soon hopefully!"

"Talk to you later, dude!" responded Marty.

DJ sat in silence for a few moments as he reviewed their conversation. He tried to come to terms with potentially not being on the same team as Marty, and the possibility was very hard on him emotionally. He thought of all the time the two had spent together at the rink and on the road. They were nearly inseparable, but now they faced a challenge that was ultimately out of their control.

CHAPTER XII

WEDNESDAY NIGHT

DJ gathered up his hockey equipment and put it all in his bag—making sure all the gear was accounted for. He zipped the bag shut, lifted it up over his shoulder and brought it out to the front door.

"Heading out, Mom," he announced to his mother, who was upstairs.

"Okay. Good luck out there tonight, DJ," she replied enthusiastically.

"Thanks, Mom. Love you!"

He picked up his sticks, which were already propped up next to the door, and left the house. His dad was waiting for him in the car. After placing his gear in the back seat of the vehicle, DJ hopped into the passenger seat.

"All set?" asked his dad.

"Sure am…" replied DJ as he pulled the seatbelt over his shoulder and across his body—fastening it into place. "Here we go!"

"Glad you are excited, son," his dad said with a smile and backed out of the driveway. They began their commute to the arena. "So, I was talking to Marty's dad…"

"Oh yeah?"

"He mentioned that Marty will be out for a while. There's no real timeline."

"Yeah," DJ responded. "We were messaging each other a bit Monday morning. He said out indefinitely with a concussion and whiplash."

"Right. His dad said he was doing alright otherwise, though," Mr. Roberts stated. "He thought maybe it would have taken a harder toll… but he has been really positive."

"That's good. He's resilient and always positive," DJ said. "Really bothers me though. We were both lights out on the weekend. Could have both easily signed… now who knows what his fate will be with the injury—because of Kip."

"Okay, let me stop you right there," Mr. Roberts told his son. "From our vantage point, it looked like Kip was just trying to finish a check—he didn't seek out the hit, it was there to be delivered. So, you need to resolve your anger toward Kip. Marty has forgiven him—so should you. Secondly, I understand your confidence, but I don't want you to feel you are entitled to one of those cards, DJ! You need to earn it. I know you had a strong showing, but stay humble and hungry!"

DJ looked somewhat ashamed of his previous statement and responded to his dad quietly. "I know. I get it…"

"I hope so, son… and—with all due respect to your friendship—you need to worry about yourself when it comes to making the team. Marty will worry about what he needs to do, and that's exactly what he was doing prior to the injury."

"Yeah…"

"I know this sounds harsh," his dad continued, "but the bottom line is that you can only control your own fate. You have personal goals and if you truly want to achieve them—which I believe you do—then you need to stay on point."

DJ understood the message his father was trying to deliver. "I get it, Dad. I just feel bad—that's all."

"I understand, son," replied Mr. Roberts. "To be honest, I was very impressed with how you handled yourself after Marty's injury on Sunday. You remained focused and were a major contributor. I am more concerned with where you are mentally: thinking you guys deserve those spots on the team. Competition is strong for both cards—even without Marty on the ice! Go out with each opportunity presented to you with the intent of proving yourself!"

"I will."

The 28 skaters and three goaltenders hit the ice and began to warm up once the Zamboni gate closed. For the first time since training camp had started, Coach Fitzgerald was on the ice, set to put the team through the paces during the evening skate. On his agenda were several battle drills, line rushes, breakouts and a mini-scrimmage to finish off.

Coach Fitzgerald blew his whistle and held his stick high in the air as he positioned himself near the timekeeper's box. Everyone made their way over to listen—half kneeled and the other half remained on their feet.

"Good evening, guys," Coach Fitzgerald began. "Tonight, we are all united in an effort to go into the Labour Day Classic as best prepared as we can be. We are all part of the Revolution—even if it's just for the immediate future! I want you guys to compete hard, but I don't want to see any liberties being taken out here tonight."

The players acknowledged the statement. "Okay, Coach."

"I don't want you guys to lose your drive out here—we are always in evaluation on this team—but we want to see every single one of you in action this weekend. So, with that being said, let's warm up the tenders. Everyone down to the end."

DJ wondered if the coach's statements were being directed to the team in regard to Marty's injury, and if anything had been said to Kip about the hit. It turned out that he wasn't the only one with that on his mind.

"Think that has anything to do with the hit on Marty?" Dozer asked as he skated alongside DJ down to the end of the rink.

"Maybe," DJ replied.

"A bit late for him," Dozer stated as they lined up to begin the drill.

Coach Fitzgerald divided the skaters into three lines and started the practice. The players got a bit of skating, puck handling, passing and shooting out of the first few drills, while the goalies were able to warm up with some shots. It wasn't long before Coach Fitzgerald signalled the end of the warm-up phase and introduced some intensity to the practice. The skaters started to feel their competitive nature being dialed up and they brought the level of their game up to match. The Coach had them go through some down-low battle drills first.

DJ was ready to go and was set to face Wallace Black in a 1-on-1 out of the corner. Black was positioned between DJ and the net, and he was set to make life difficult for the young winger as he tried to make it to the goal with the puck. On the whistle, DJ darted off the wall and turned from his start position facing the boards. Black was forced to start from goalpost. The two engaged in action near the bottom of the faceoff circle and DJ looked to slide the puck through the monstrous defenceman's legs and dodge the contact. Wallace Black's strong stick met the puck before DJ could attempt his move, ending the play abruptly.

DJ returned to the lineup, frustrated with his effort. It wasn't long until he got a chance to redeem his first attempt—this time he would face Victor Sharp. The whistle sounded again and DJ burst out of the corner. Sharp was a great skater and very agile. From their time playing on the same team together, the two had entered many similar battles in practices and each knew the other's tendencies really well. DJ drove out higher this time and got a bit of a step on the defender. Protecting the puck on his backhand, DJ lowered his shoulder and leaned on Sharp as he broke toward the net. It was a good battle of strength between the two, and as DJ drew closer to the net he managed to get off a tame shot that was easily turned away by Carter Riddle in net.

"Nice battle, DJ," complimented Victor Sharp as he skated away.

"Thanks, Sharpie... you too!" Truth be told, DJ wasn't happy with his effort and felt as though there was a microscope placed upon him, evaluating each and every aspect of his game. "C'mon, DJ!" he said to himself as he returned to the line once again.

Practice continued to move along and DJ's night just wasn't quite to the standard he had established for himself. During the line rushes, he felt the pressure even more so when he had a few of his plays broken up early. Everything that had gone right on the weekend seemed to be working against him here on Wednesday night.

"Man, I'm struggling," announced DJ as he lined up next to Joel Stevenson.

"Don't be so hard on yourself, man," Dozer said compassionately. "You'll bounce back!"

"Thanks, Dozer," DJ responded, but even the kind words from his friend couldn't ease the tension building inside of him.

"Just keep working, buddy," sounded Kip Kelley as he skated up behind the two standing in the corner. "A few rough plays aren't going to define you out here, DJ. They know what you're capable of!"

DJ was surprised once again by Kip. "Thanks, Kip. I appreciate that."

The words from Kip helped relieve some of DJ's stress and he was able to collect his thoughts. He tried to focus on the upcoming task—a 3-on-2 with Brendan Burrow and Dozer—and think less about who was watching and what they were thinking of his performance.

The three forwards began their next play against the defensive tandem of Andrew Boersman and Cody Ryerson. Burrow skated up the middle of the ice with the puck and passed it to the left side. DJ controlled the puck and pressured Ryerson with some speed on the outside. He broke in over the blueline and returned a drop pass back to Burrow. Burrow received the pass and fired a hard-low shot at Edward Boushy in net. The shot bounced off the goalie's left pad and came to lie just outside the crease on the right side of the goal. Dozer was barrelling in toward the loose puck and successfully fought off Boersman to tap the puck into the gaping net. The three forwards came together and celebrated with a few high-fives.

"There you go, DJ!" shouted Dozer. "Now you're going!"

A weight was truly lifted off DJ's shoulders from that moment going forward in the skate. The rest of Coach Fitzgerald's planned drills wrapped up and now they would use the remaining 20 minutes to have a mini-scrimmage between Team Navy and Team Silver.

DJ's line started on the bench and watched as Kip Kelley faced off with JJ Turcotte. Kip controlled the play from the drop of the puck and Team Navy put on some initial pressure to start the game. Turcotte's line was hemmed in the defensive zone for the first minute of play before managing to escape the zone and get the puck in deep so they could perform a line change.

Over the boards came the trio of DJ, Burrow and Dozer. They began the shift on the defensive side of the puck as Stewart Cooke and the rest of Team Navy had already transitioned into the offensive zone. Cooke had a pair of powerful wingers with him and the unit worked the puck low on Team Silver. James Northgate and Mike McDennis made life difficult for Andrew Boersman and Cody Ryerson, but the steady work from Burrow made the difference—he was able to pin McDennis on the wall and create a turnover. Ryerson picked up the puck and passed it up to Dozer on the half wall. A quick touch-pass into the middle sprung DJ as he came across in support of his right winger.

Eric Matheson and Donald Redman retreated as the winger broke out on the attack. DJ skated hard up the ice, but he had no support as he took on the defensive tandem alone. He gained the redline and chipped the puck in behind Matheson—then jumped around him and raced after the loose puck. Redman pivoted at the same time and closed in on the puck. His long stick managed to poke the puck away and down into the corner, but DJ stayed on it and gained control.

Now his linemates were able to get back into the play, however, DJ didn't have much time so he cycled the puck in behind the net and into the far corner. Burrow was breaking down the middle and charged in. He was played closely by Matheson, but saw Dozer coming in to help. Burrow bounced the puck off the boards to Dozer in behind the net. The big winger controlled it and made a hard move to the front of the net. He slung the puck hard as he stepped out above the goal line, but Riddle was already set and trapped the shot.

Coach Fitzgerald—acting as the referee—blew his whistle and came in to pick up the puck for a faceoff. "Nice work, Silver!" he said as he approached front of the net.

DJ, Burrow and Dozer were pulled off the ice, but were happy with their performance on the shift. The scrimmage didn't have quite the same energy as the two intersquad games on the weekend, but the players were giving everything they had. DJ took in each and every play—whether he was on the ice or on the bench. He watched as Scott Parker from Team Navy broke up a cross-ice play from Matt Manson to Wallace Black—the speedy winger skated in uncontested and buried a shot five-hole on Edward Boushy.

Then, on the very next shift, DJ watched newcomer Trent Rosenberg closely from the bench. Rosenberg had been somewhat quiet up to this point, but DJ witnessed what made the right winger so dangerous. Working on a line with Dominic O'Connor and Kip Kelley, Rosenberg patrolled the high slot as his Team Navy linemates dominated deep. Kip broke away from his check and spotted Rosenberg's stick cocked high—signalling for a pass. Kip made a nice, flat saucer pass out of the corner, over the defender's stick and Rosenberg connected on the one-timer. The shot blasted into the goal and gave Team Navy a 2–0 lead.

Spencer McIntyre relieved Edward Boushy in Team Silver's goal for the last half of the scrimmage. Boushy had played well, but he couldn't stop the two fabulous scoring chances that had been directed at him.

Team Silver was able to create some pressure to begin the last half of the scrimmage, but Riddle made all of his saves look routine. DJ, alone, had three shots during that stretch of play. Play continued and Trent Rosenberg made his presence felt once again when he received a breakaway pass from Victor Sharp on a stretch play. Rosenberg cheated his own zone as he anticipated a turnover—a play that he read correctly. Upon receiving the pass from Sharp, Rosenberg moved in on McIntyre and ripped home a wrist shot over the blocker of the southpaw—bringing the score to 3–0 Team Navy.

DJ looked on in admiration at the release Rosenberg had displayed on both of his goals. "Wow! Those were impressive goals," he said to the linemates next to him on the bench.

They didn't have much time to talk about it as they were back over the boards trying to break the goose egg currently held by Carter Riddle. This was likely their last chance to do so, as time was closing in on the end of practice.

Off the faceoff, Brendan Burrow overpowered his opponent and gained possession for Team Silver. Wallace Black looked to make a quick play up to DJ on the wing, but was forced into having to chip it off the glass as he was pressured quickly by Dominic O'Connor. O'Connor had burst in from the far side and was looking to strip the big defender. DJ was lined up against Rosenberg and the two battled on the wall as the puck bounced toward Team Navy's blueline. DJ was able to slide the puck deep into the offensive zone.

Dallas Freeman went back to pick up the puck and shovelled it behind the net to his partner as Burrow took away his lane. Sharp controlled the puck, but he was also forced quickly by Dozer. Dozer managed to stop the defender before he could move the puck and the two engaged in a down-low battle for possession. In the middle of the ice, Kip dropped down to help Sharp and managed to gain control of the puck—DJ moved in and had Kip in perfect position to lay a check.

Thoughts of revenge ran through DJ's mind as he knew that he could deliver a thunderous blow to the person who had taken out his best friend. As he came in, the discussion with his dad and Coach Fitzgerald's declaration at the beginning of the skate echoed through his mind. DJ turned his focus to the puck—and stripped Kip of it.

As he turned up the boards, he saw Burrow streaking toward the goal from the opposite corner. DJ shot the puck hard into the slot. Burrow connected with his stick and as the goaltender slid laterally, Burrow redirected the puck back through Riddle's legs and broke the shutout. The skaters came together in celebration, but that was as close as they could bring the scrimmage, as Team Navy held on for a 3–1 victory.

Coach Fitzgerald held a final huddle at centre ice while the players stretched. "Great skate tonight, fellas. Let's carry on this weekend and show the other teams at the tournament that we should not be taken lightly this season! We start Friday night at 6:00 pm against the Hawks. If for some reason you are unable to play, let me know. Otherwise, I would like everyone to be there ready to go! The lineup will not be announced until you get there. We are guaranteed to play three games, and I want to see everyone in at least one. Any questions?"

The players looked around—nobody had anything to say.

"Alright, guys. We'll see you Friday," announced Coach Fitzgerald.

CHAPTER XIII

A DAY AWAY

"Hey… didn't see you at the skate last night. Did you get over to the arena?" DJ sent a text to his best friend. After they had talked about it, DJ had anticipated seeing Marty out at the practice but he didn't spot him before, during or after. He wondered if he missed him or if something had prevented Marty from making it out.

DJ planned to use Thursday as a bit of a rest day—he intended to go to the gym for a light cardio session but nothing overly intense. He was in the middle of watching the morning sports highlights when he heard a new message alert on his phone.

Marty replied, *"Morning, DJ. Wanted to make it out, but have been suffering from headaches when I get up and move around. Unfortunately couldn't get out to watch. How did things go?"*

"It went alright… bit of a rough start for me but I picked it up as things went along."

"That's good. Looking forward to the weekend I assume? Do you know what games you are playing in yet?" questioned Marty.

"Looking forward to it that's for sure! No idea what games I'll be in," DJ informed his friend. *"Coach wants everyone to be ready for action Friday night… but the lineup won't be available till then."*

"Right on… I will try to get down if I'm doing better!" responded Marty. *"I get re-evaluated during the day tomorrow. Hope the news is good!"*

"Same here! Good luck buddy!"

"Thanks. I really appreciate the support!" replied Marty gratefully. *"So, any standouts from last night? Who were you playing with?"* As long as DJ had known Marty he had always been a hockey buff and craved as many details as he could get, even during this rough time.

"New player back from Ottawa named Trent Rosenberg scored two beauties… he lined up with Kipper and O'Connor. I was with Burrow and Dozer."

"Nice. Sounds like two good lines there!"

"Yeah… Dozer is a natural and Burrow has been easy to play with. Plays a solid but simple game," wrote DJ as he gave a general synopsis of his linemates.

"That's great! It's awesome when you have guys that you mesh well with immediately," replied Marty enthusiastically. *"But I need to get showered and dressed… heading out shortly to get some school materials… FUN! lol"*

DJ chuckled at his friend's sarcasm. *"Haha… indeed! Well hopefully you don't have any issues with your headaches that would prevent you from doing that! ;) ;)"*

"LOL! Should I play it up?" wrote Marty jokingly. *"Talk to you later, dude!"*

"Later!"

Down at the The Coffee Shop, the Revolution staff assembled to go over the particulars of the upcoming tournament—most importantly the lineup for the first game against the Hawks. This topic created some debate, as the Hawks were one of the top teams in the league and had many returning skaters. They had added the Anderson twins to the mix, meaning they would likely have less talent to analyze in the Friday night matchup than the Revolution would. The Hawks would probably be icing a veteran-heavy lineup. That possibility created an internal debate between the staff on how to put together their group.

"We need to evaluate our unsigned skaters as much as possible," commented GM Flaherty.

"I understand this, Bob! But do we want to take a whipping in our first game, or do we want to show a team like the Hawks that we are capable of competing?" Coach Fitzgerald questioned strongly.

"I know it is concerning—either way," replied GM Flaherty calmly. "We either see how our prospects handle the situation *or* we deliver our top guys and send a statement. For me, my strategy is to hide my hand and let that unfold the first time we meet them in the season. Let's see how the remaining guys respond to the challenge."

Assistant GM Chambers added to the discussion. "We still have to implement some strong players into the lineup regardless, based on our number situation."

"That's right, Doug," agreed GM Flaherty. "That Burrow, Roberts and Stevenson line looked strong last night; I would have those three together again."

"Could see what Cooke and O'Connor bring," added Assistant GM Chambers.

"Okay," responded Coach Fitzgerald. "I guess that is probably the best way to approach the game."

"Alright," said GM Flaherty as they settled the issue. "I'll leave you to your lineup!"

The three members of the Revolution staff continued their conversation. They talked about the five underage skaters that would be in the lineup during the tournament—and of course Brad Martinsen and how to manage his situation. They discussed how their positional needs could potentially influence their decision regarding that matter as well. Presently, the team had signed two left wingers, three centres, three right wingers, one left-handed defenceman and three right-handed defencemen.

Adding to the depth up front was new arrival Trent Rosenberg. Should Rosenberg and the team come to terms, it would create a very strong right side—potentially forcing one of the skaters to play on their off-wing or in the middle. That would create a tough task for the four hopeful forwards. Leading the pack after a strong weekend would be DJ Roberts—theoretically. However, both Brendan Burrow and Mike McDennis were strong performers as well. The uncertainty around Brad Martinsen and his status could very well leave him from being part of the discussion altogether.

Taking this into account, the Revolution staff could look at Victor Sharp and Eric Matheson closely for the underage positions. Needing some depth on defence, the two left-handed shooters would provide the team with a solid top six. Prospectively pairing them with sturdy partners Freeman and Black could be very lucrative for their development. The staff looked at all angles as conversation continued, but they knew their answers would unfold during the tournament.

CHAPTER XIV

GM#1 > REVOLUTION VS HAWKS

The big day had finally arrived and DJ could hardly wait to get to the arena. He had a tough time getting to bed the night before, but he was able to sleep in and ensure that he was well rested heading into the first game of the Labour Day Classic Tournament—should he be called upon to play. Having yet to sign, DJ figured he would be a lock in the lineup tonight as the team would want to see how the underagers compared against the tough competition.

DJ arrived at the arena to get ready for the game at 4:15 pm. He raced into the building and sought out where the Revolution would be dressing—Room One. Once he had that information he made his way toward the room. As he approached the dressing room he could see a sheet of paper taped to the door. Just as he suspected, it was tonight's lineup.

GM#1 VS THE HAWKS

Dominic O'Connor – Stewart Cooke – Jeremy Wright
DJ Roberts – Brendan Burrow – Mike McDennis
Justin Norris – Steve Reinhart – Scott Parker
Anson Brown – Kole Kelley – Matt Manson

Victor Sharp – Cody Ryerson
Eric Matheson – Matthew MacKenzie
Andrew Boersman – Martin Killington

Spencer McIntyre
Edward Boushy

DJ found himself alongside two other underage candidates in Burrow and McDennis. In Burrow he had found some immediate chemistry and in McDennis he had a renowned history of success. In his mind, he knew they were in competition, but also knew that they would help each other's game. DJ was very optimistic as he returned to the vehicle to grab his hockey bag and sticks.

"Playing tonight?" asked his dad as DJ opened the door.

"With Burrow and McDennis," he replied eagerly.

"Sounds like a good line!" his dad responded. "I'll see you on the ice. Good luck!"

"Thanks, Dad!"

DJ made his way back to the dressing room. He was one of the first players there and began to get himself mentally and physically ready. The coaching staff was scattered around the room and in the hallway prior to warm-ups—periodically Assistant Coaches McIntosh or Horton would begin a conversation with an individual or a group of players.

They were going over a little in-game strategy and some detail work.

Coach McIntosh called DJ, Burrow and McDennis out into the hallway. As the skaters left the dressing room with the assistant coach, they were met by Coach Fitzgerald in the hall.

"Gentlemen," Coach Fitzgerald greeted them. "As you have seen, you three will be playing together tonight at even strength. You will also be running as our second power-play unit. DJ and Brendan... I will be using you together on the penalty kill, as well."

"Sounds good, Coach," the three replied.

"This is a big matchup for us tonight," Coach Fitzgerald continued. "The Hawks have their team pretty well picked and are going to be using this weekend to prepare for the season. Our team, on the other hand, is using it more as an evaluation process. They will likely have a lot of veterans playing—I will know more when the game sheet comes our way. You three guys are all young, but I don't want you to feel outmatched. What I have seen from you—you guys can play at this level. This is your chance to make an impression. This is your chance to show you belong! Let's have a good one, guys!"

"Thanks, Coach," responded the three young skaters and they turned back into the room to finish getting ready.

Not long after the trio re-entered the dressing room, the entire team was summoned out onto the ice to partake in warm-ups. The warm-ups in the tournament were eight minutes in duration and would lead directly into the first period of action—unlike the traditional warm-ups they would have during the regular season.

The players were excited as they hit the ice, and it showed as they went through the paces before the game.

Passes were sharp, shots were on target and the goalies were patrolling the crease with precision. DJ felt loose and full of energy as he worked through the warm-up regimen. He took a moment to collect his thoughts and scope the crowd of people that were out to witness the action. He noticed a fair-sized gathering out to watch—mostly parents, but also a good number of dedicated fans supporting the Hawks.

BUZZ...

The score clock's buzzer sounded to end the warm-up and both teams stopped and proceeded to their bench to prepare for the opening faceoff.

"Alright, guys," Coach Fitzgerald said as he addressed his team. "We know we are going to be in tough against a strong team, but that is why we show up each and every day! We crave competition! We didn't come here to take the easy road and that goes for the entire season. We came here to work. We came here to improve and better ourselves, each and every moment possible. You may not all suit up for the Revolution this upcoming season, but we will always have this moment together—as a team. Now let's go out there and show what we are made of! Cooke's line—start things off!"

Prior to both teams hitting the ice, Coach Fitzgerald became privy to the Hawks' lineup. One quick glance at the roster they were icing and he knew that the Revolution would be in for a difficult matchup. Their opponent's starting three would be Jason Clermont, Cole Reese and newly acquired Kyler Lite—their projected first line for the year. Clermont had led the team in goals and points last year, while Reese had led in assists. The two would be accompanied by a twenty-year-old making his way back from Major Junior in Guelph. Lite was an intimidating force—listed at 6′4″ and 200 lbs—and provided scoring to go along with his big frame. Added to the mix was the Hawks' leading defensive scorer, Nick Wager. Wager played well in all situations and was a catalyst for the top power-play unit.

Of the 18 skaters the Hawks would be using tonight, only 7 were unsigned—compared to 15 for the Revolution. Nevertheless, they were ready to take on the formidable challenge.

Stewart Cooke moved in for the opening faceoff against Clermont. The referee inched inward and gestured to both goaltenders to confirm they were ready to begin. He returned his focus to the faceoff dot and released the puck from his hand. It seemed to echo thunderously as it hit the ice. Cooke and Clermont engaged with their sticks, with Clermont coming away with the win. He sent it back to Wager and the first game of the Labour Day Classic Tournament was underway.

The Hawks applied pressure right of the hop—and were very poised and controlled as they did it. They set the tempo, and they set it at a rapid pace. The Revolution had played intensely during their intersquad games, but it was evident that they would need to dig in even deeper tonight.

The line of Cooke, O'Connor and Wright luckily escaped the first shift unscathed, and were able to make a line change on-the-fly after putting the puck deep into the offensive zone. DJ, Burrow and McDennis were next in line and made their way over the boards to take on the next wave of attack from the Hawks.

Leading the rush was Nolan Anderson—the underage centre. Joining him on the rush was his twin brother and the two burst up the ice with flash. The twins were met by their rival forwards and were forced to send the puck into the corner. Spencer McIntyre came out to meet the puck as it whipped around the boards, and he stopped it for Eric Matheson behind the net.

"Middle! Middle!" DJ hollered as he found a gap in the defensive zone.

Matheson took a quick step out, away from pressure, and sent a hard pass to DJ's stick. DJ gathered the puck and turned up ice—but he was being marked the entire way by the Hawks' defence. Mark Brown stepped up inside the blueline and made a check on the winger that allowed Nathan Anderson to gain control in the offensive zone.

Nathan Anderson circled in and spotted his brother driving to the net from the corner. Without hesitation, Nathan sent a hard pass and Nolan found himself with a quality scoring chance early in the game. He controlled the puck and picked his spot, however, Spencer McIntyre tracked the puck perfectly with his glove and held on for a whistle.

A relieved DJ went down to praise his goaltender for bailing him out. "Great save, Spence! Sorry about that."

"All good," the netminder responded to his forward confidently.

While the score remained 0–0, the shot total was growing increasingly different by the minute. By the halfway mark of the first period, the Hawks led 12-to-3 in shots, signifying the lopsided play on the ice.

"We've got to sharpen up out there, guys," urged Coach Fitzgerald. "Too many turnovers and too many forced plays! Keep it simple! Get it deep and go to work!"

The Revolution skaters were watching from the bench—witnessing exactly what the coach was referring to. They collectively struggled to find any flow and were getting hemmed up in their own end for long durations.

"Let's step it up here," proclaimed DJ as he sat with Burrow and McDennis on the bench. "We've got more to offer!"

Unfortunately, they would have to wait a few shifts before getting a chance to act, as Matthew MacKenzie was receiving a two-minute penalty for roughing after the whistle. Cooke and O'Connor were called upon to begin the kill up front and would be joined by Sharp and Ryerson.

Jason Clermont won the faceoff to begin the power play, which led to offensive control for the Hawks. Wager received the puck and positioned himself at the top of the zone and the power-play unit moved into a 1-3-1 formation. Wager moved the puck with Clermont, who then used Reese down in the corner. The three talented Hawks worked the puck well and looked to open up Kyler Lite in the slot for a one-time attempt.

The Revolution took away any good looks for Lite in the middle, which led to the power-play unit implementing more movement with their attack. Clermont slid the puck down to Reese once again and darted in front of the net. Sharp read the give-and-go and stuck with Clermont— allowing Reese to move into some open space. As Reese skated up, he maintained his vision and spotted the shifty Greg Monroe sneaking in on the backdoor. Reese sent the cross-crease pass instantly, and Monroe bashed in the puck to make the game 1–0.

The Hawks' faithful fans and bench cheered loudly as the power-play unit gathered beside the net and celebrated the opening goal. Spencer McIntyre pulled the puck from in behind and shot it toward centre—showing his frustration following the goal against.

"Going to be a long night for you, buddy," yelled Kyler Lite arrogantly as he skated passed McIntyre.

The quick power-play goal against prevented DJ and Burrow from getting on the ice to kill the penalty, so their line was called upon to make a response.

"Get one back for Spence here now!" DJ called to his linemates as they hopped the boards.

Burrow outmuscled Nolan Anderson on the following faceoff and the Revolution were able to get the puck behind the defence and go on the attack. However, the slick Nick Wager gathered up the puck and made an effortless outlet pass to relieve any form of pressure.

DJ found himself burning a lot of energy as he raced back and forth, but his efforts were unproductive and uncharacteristic. His actions were replicated by his teammates, and they struggled to gain any traction as the first period came to a close. Spencer McIntyre played strongly in net, but a point shot was deflected in during the last minute and the Revolution found themselves down 2–0 heading into the intermission—being outshot 19-to-6.

Between periods, the players were very quiet as they sat in the dressing room. The team was deflated and felt mentally defeated. Coach Fitzgerald entered the room.

"Guys," he began, "it isn't pretty out there—that's the truth. However, the deficit is two goals. Erase that period from your memory and prepare to begin the next. I know you have more in you to give… much more. You know they are good and it showed. Don't let them get in your head! You guys are on the ice with them so go be the difference maker!"

The little pep talk allowed the players to regain their concentration and the energy level slowly grew as the second period drew closer. The starting lines remained the same on both sides of the ice, and Stewart Cooke and company looked to interrupt the momentum the Hawks had obtained. Cooke edged out Clermont on the opening faceoff and Victor Sharp dished the puck quickly over to Cody Ryerson. Cole Reese bolted toward Ryerson and limited his options, so he settled for a chip off the wall toward Jeremy Wright. Wright secured the puck and shot it into the offensive zone.

The Hawks' goaltender, 6'5" Christian MacLean, left his net and stopped the puck for Nick Wager. Wager used a quick touch to elude Cooke and sent the puck to his partner. Victor Jeffrey took control in his own zone, but he was closed in on by Dominic O'Connor who was able to poke the puck loose. O'Connor skated onto the puck, but Jeffrey laid a heavy slash on the forward. O'Connor was dropped by the dirty stick infraction, and Wager touched the puck to stop the play on the upcoming penalty call.

O'Connor got back to his feet and was engaged in a bit of a pushing match with Jeffrey, but the Revolution forward knew better and skated away. Cooke, O'Connor and Wright began the power play on forward, but they were shut down effectively.

Next up were DJ, Burrow and McDennis. They took over the power play at approximately the minute mark and fell back with Eric Matheson and Martin Killington to breakout from their own zone. Matheson led the way and as he gained pressure, he sent a pass to DJ up the left side.

DJ flew up the wing and was well supported. The Hawks limited his space as he crossed the blueline—forcing DJ to rim the puck around the end wall. McDennis skated hard to the oncoming puck, and absorbed contact from the opposing defence as he let the puck continue by him. The fluid-skating Killington retrieved the puck on the wall and opened up into the middle of the ice. Killington worked the puck with Sharp on the backend while the forwards positioned themselves properly. Using very similar tactics as the Hawks had on their power play, the Revolution had DJ on the half wall, Burrow down low, and McDennis in the slot.

Killington pivoted and used DJ on his right side, looking to shift the penalty killers to open up lanes. DJ read it beautifully and one-touched the puck to McDennis in the high slot. McDennis made no mistake on the shot—sending a rocket at the tall goalie. MacLean dropped instinctively as McDennis connected, but the tall goaltender couldn't stop the shot as it grazed the crossbar on its way into the net.

The goal brought a surge of energy to the Revolution on the ice and on the bench. DJ raced in to celebrate with McDennis—as did the others on the ice.

"That's what I'm talking about!" shouted Killington as he joined the huddle.

"Nice work, guys!" announced Sharp. "Great shot, Mickey-D!"

The Revolution were lifted and it was reflected in their game as the second period moved forward. Line after line, the team continued to buzz and create shots. At the five-minute mark, they had already reached their first period output in shots. While the Revolution's game had certainly picked up, the Hawks remained steady at both ends of the ice. Spencer McIntyre finished off the first half of the game in goal before swapping places with Edward Boushy. As McIntyre made his way to the bench, he looked at the score clock and saw that he had allowed two goals on 24 shots against. The referee allotted Boushy a few minutes to prepare himself in the Revolution net before play resumed.

On the following faceoff, the Hawks were able to gain control and looked to test the new goaltender early. The Anderson twins cycled the puck deep in the corner and created some good looks, but Boushy appeared ready for action and was able to adjust to the pace.

The relentless pressure from the Hawks still caused problems for the Revolution in the defensive zone. Matt

Manson approached Nick Wager on the point and looked like he wanted to make contact on the Hawk defender. Wager deked around Manson, however, Manson tripped him on his way by. Manson made his way to the penalty box due to the infraction.

The Clermont power-play unit emerged onto the ice and moved the puck around beautifully, once again. Clermont worked the puck with Reese beside the goal, and then found Kyler Lite on a one-time attempt in the slot. The shot beat Boushy to the stick side—creating a 3–1 advantage for the Hawks.

The following faceoff resulted in a scrambled draw. Nathan Anderson broke into the middle to help his brother and retrieved the puck ahead of his checker. He slid the puck through the legs of an oncoming opponent—making a pass to Kurtis Alderidge on the left side. Alderidge was a big, strong skater and was able to get on the outside of Martin Killington and outpower the smaller defender. Using his strength, Alderidge barrelled in on Boushy and pulled the puck across the top of the crease, onto his backhand and buried the goal—moving the Hawks ahead by three to finish the period.

The third period was more of the same. The Clermont line dominated and potted two more goals in the first ten minutes of the period. Jason Clermont was now up to four assists in the game. The Hawks remained tight defensively as the period wore on, but in the dying minutes of the game, Kole Kelley made a tremendous individual effort around the Hawks' defence and scored the final goal of the game. The Hawks won 6–2, outshooting the Revolution 46-to-27.

CHAPTER XV

SCOUTING THE OPPONENT

Up in the stands, Coach Fitzgerald and his staff sat amongst the spectators as the Hawks and Raiders took to the ice for their 12:00 pm clash on Saturday. The coaches knew they went into Friday night's matchup blind, and they were not going to consciously make that mistake again in their evening game with the Raiders. On top of learning what to expect from their forthcoming opponent, they were interested in the outcome. Should the Hawks win once again, the Revolution and Raiders showdown would determine second spot in their pool—with the winner playing for third overall on Sunday. But if the Raiders were able to win in regulation, the pool would remain wide open and would depend on the result of the evening battle—creating a window of opportunity for the Revolution to play for first overall.

"Looks like the Clermont line is resting after taking it to us last night," exclaimed Assistant Coach Horton.

"They're out," replied Coach Fitzgerald. "As well as Wager. Looks like London, Richmond and Bouchard slotted in up front and Pillman and Case on the point."

"Look at the size of Case!" announced an astonished Assistant Coach McIntosh. "The guy is huge." He was referring to second year defender Brandon Case, who was a staggering 6'6".

"What was the final score in the Jaguars versus Black Knights game last night?" Assistant Coach Horton asked out of curiosity.

"Eight to three final, for the Jags," responded Coach Fitzgerald. "It was close enough until the last half of the third period, then the Jags popped in three unanswered goals to finish them off."

The game began as the three coaches conversed in the crowd. They kept a close eye on the action and noticed that the Hawks, even without their big line, were still dominating their competition early on in the tournament.

"Well, I don't feel quite as bad after watching the Raiders go through the same treatment we faced," proclaimed Assistant Coach Horton.

"How did you guys feel about our game last night?" asked Coach Fitzgerald. He was interested in their reflections after having some time to reassess the game overnight.

"Terrible defensively," stated Assistant Coach Horton. "It was an absolute nightmare trying to breakout. Take that blunder out of our game and we may have been able to amount to more offensively."

"I agree," said Assistant Coach McIntosh. "You could see our inexperience, in my opinion. A few team practices and a chance for the young guys that will be sticking around to get their feet wet, and I believe that will begin to straighten out."

"Personally," Coach Fitzgerald began, "I felt the Cooke line was overmatched; the Burrow line was awestruck; and our bottom two lines just flat out couldn't compete. On the backend we lacked patience with the puck, in general. Spencer McIntyre may have been the lone bright spot of the game. He plainly and simply gave us a chance while he was in net and when Boushy entered, he didn't."

"That's blunt," responded Assistant Coach McIntosh with a quick chuckle. "But it's a fair insight. We were missing some key components which would allow us to peg people into their correct place though."

"I'm not suggesting that we aren't," replied Coach Fitzgerald firmly. "I just expected a little bit more from our lineup. I was disappointed in the showing."

"So," Assistant Coach Horton started, "what did we learn about what we have?"

"We learned we are inexperienced," said Assistant Coach McIntosh.

"We learned that the Hawks—and the other top teams in this league—are unforgiving and will clean you if you aren't ready to go," commented Coach Fitzgerald candidly.

"Individually, I liked what I saw from Victor Sharp and Martin Killington. Up front, the players with the biggest impact were McDennis and Kole Kelley—and that was really only because of their superb goals. Roberts had a nice assist, but he looked too frantic. Burrow was steady, although he looked a step behind. Parker was flying, however he wasn't able to mesh with his linemates."

"I thought Matheson played decently on the back end," added Assistant Coach Horton. "He was probably my pick for best defensively."

"I'll give you that," Coach Fitzgerald admitted. "Compared to Sharp though—overall game just wasn't there."

Out on the ice, the Hawks had opened up the scoring with a power play marker and followed it up with another strike at 5-on-5. They took a 2–0 lead into the first intermission—just like in last night's game against the Revolution.

"What type of lineup are you putting together for later on?" asked Assistant Coach McIntosh. "Bringing in everyone that didn't play last night?"

"There will be a little bit of a shakeup," replied Coach Fitzgerald. "In all likelihood, we will be battling for the chance to play for third on Sunday, which should mean facing stronger competition. We have some guys that we need to look at further in this next game, so some of our top guys may need to stay out until then… but I will put some more thought into it later."

"Sounds good," responded the two assistants.

The crew watched the rest of the game, taking as many notes as possible. The Hawks were starting to open up the game and took a 4–1 lead into the third period of play. Drew Marshall was between the pipes for the Hawks' second game and was another key piece for the strong team. While MacLean played solidly for them the previous night, Marshall was a talented goaltender coming off a strong rookie year and was the projected starter.

In the third period, the Raiders were able to score twice on the power play—converting on a 5-on-3 advantage, and then on the following 5-on-4 advantage to bring the game back within reach. As play continued, the Raiders' momentum fizzled and then disappeared when Nathan Anderson scored on a breakaway to restore a two-goal lead.

An empty-net goal iced the game and the Hawks defeated the Raiders 6–3 to earn first place in their pool. The Revolution staff now knew that their next matchup would determine who would go on to battle for third overall in the tournament—an accomplishment that would look good for the inaugural team.

CHAPTER XVI

GM#2 > REVOLUTION VS RAIDERS

The Revolution started to arrive at the arena for their second game of the tournament. As the players made their way to the dressing room, they saw that once again, Coach Fitzgerald had left a sheet of paper with the lineup posted on the door.

<u>GM#2 vs The Raiders</u>

DJ Roberts – Kip Kelley – Trent Rosenberg
Harrison Gage – JJ Turcotte – James Northgate
Mike McDennis – Kole Kelley – Joel Stevenson
Anson Brown – Steve Reinhart – Scott Parker

Victor Sharp – Curtis Kraemer
Eric Matheson – Donald Freeman
Andrew Boersman – Martin Killington

Edward Boushy
Spencer McIntyre

The lineup was a much heavier veteran lineup up front compared to the previous night, but with the many question marks surrounding the team's defensive depth, their most experienced defenders, Wallace Black and Dallas Freeman, were left out of the lineup. Also, as sure as Coach Fitzgerald was with the direction he wanted to go with his backup goalie, he needed to see Boushy and McIntyre split the net once again. As a result, Carter Riddle would join the two veteran back end leaders in the stands for a second straight night.

In the dressing room, a few Revolution players gathered to talk about the team and what had happened so far in the tournament.

"Hawks won again earlier," announced Kip to a surrounding crowd of players, "so if we beat the Raiders, we will play tomorrow at 3:00 pm for third overall."

"We should have used a stronger lineup last night," stated JJ Turcotte smugly. "We could have beaten those guys and played for first tomorrow!"

"Easier said than done, JJ," replied Steve Reinhart. "Those guys were really good, man! It's not like we didn't have a decent group playing."

"Meh…" responded Turcotte. "They worked hard, but they didn't seem that skilled."

"That's what you saw? Really?" Reinhart asked in astonishment.

"Hey, at least we'll catch them by surprise when we meet in the season!" Turcotte laughed arrogantly.

"Whatever, man!" said Reinhart, who had grown frustrated with his teammate. He broke away from the conversation to get dressed.

As time rolled along, the players got ready and were soon waiting patiently in the dressing room for the cue to go out. DJ sat close in proximity to his two linemates and the three of them discussed some strategy until Assistant Coach McIntosh came in to announce the ice was ready. The Revolution hit the ice and were raring to go. Kip Kelley led the team through warm-up and ran it very effectively in the shortened time. The buzzer sounded and the players at both ends of the rink skated to their respective benches.

"Okay, guys," Coach Fitzgerald addressed his team. "New game... new faces! For those of you who were in the game last night, understand what you need to do to be better. For those of you entering the lineup, know that I expect much more than what I got from our game with the Hawks. You have a chance to beat this team—take it!"

"Here we go, boys!" yelled Kip. "Let's fire this thing up and get the jump on them quick!" The team rallied behind their top centre and they had generated some positive energy as they entered into the opening faceoff.

The line of Kip, DJ and Rosenberg moved in for the start of the game with Victor Sharp and Curtis Kraemer backing them up. Kip squared off with the Raiders' top line centre, Greg McMahon. McMahon led the sixth-seeded squad with 32 goals in 48 games played as a 17-year-old last season. To his left was Miles Newman, the team's point leader, and on his right was Ryder Parrish—this first line reunited from last year.

Kip and McMahon battled on the draw, resulting in a scramble to begin the game. DJ moved in quickly with his counterpart, Parrish, and dug for the puck. DJ was able to chip the puck out and back to Sharp, earning the Revolution the first possession of the hockey game.

The top lines duked it out for the better part of the opening minute before being relieved by the second line. The teams were playing very wide open, and both sides were able to create some scoring chances off the rush. However, both Edward Boushy and Raiders' netminder Jeremy Vaux were equal to the task; they kept the score at 0–0 through the first half of the period.

The Raiders' line of McMahon, Newman and Parrish hit the ice on-the-fly and found themselves in a good matchup against the Revolution's fourth line. The trio of Reinhart, Brown and Parker was a hard working line, but the skill level of their opposition created difficulties for them as they worked the puck deep in the Revolution zone.

McMahon cycled down low with Newman as they isolated Matheson in the corner. Watching his defenceman struggling to contain the offence, Reinhart entered into action and tried to force a turnover—but as he tried to contain the quick-skating Miles Newman, he tripped up the winger and drew the attention of the referee. Donald Redman slid away from the front of the net to touch the loose puck—and the whistle went.

"White—number eight!" the ref shouted as he pointed at Reinhart. "Two minutes for tripping!" Reinhart lowered his head and made his way to the sin bin to serve his penalty.

The McMahon line stayed on the ice for the upcoming power play. Kip and DJ were sent out and over the boards to join Matheson and Redman and kill off the start of the penalty. Kip won the draw cleanly back to Matheson in the corner on the faceoff, and Matheson was able to rip the puck hard off the glass and out of the defensive zone.

The Raiders' captain, Doug McCallister, raced back to pick up the puck in his own zone and retreated in behind the net to escape some pressure from DJ. McCallister waited for his teammates to circle back and begin their power play breakout. As the group turned up the ice, the captain moved out and skated up the middle of the defensive zone—drawing in pressure from Kip. McCallister lured the Revolution centre in and dished the puck off to Newman who was skating up on his left.

"Step up! Step up!" Coach Fitzgerald screamed at Redman as the speedy winger took control of the puck. Redman heard the plea from his coach, took a hard stride and used his great reach to disengage the puck from Newman's stick. The puck was swept back in the opposite direction—right toward Kip who had curled off McCallister.

Kip embraced the puck, slammed on the brakes, and dug in to go on the attack. DJ watched the play unfold and worked hard to get up the ice to join his centre on the rush. McCallister was the lone Raider back and he held the middle of the ice. He was well aware of both Revolution skaters' positions as they closed in on the goal. Kip glanced over at DJ, realized the passing lane was obstructed and took aim at goaltender Jeremy Vaux. Vaux had strongly positioned himself for the shot, so Kip decided to throw a quick shot along the ice—knowing a rebound opportunity could open up for his pressing winger. Vaux dropped down into the butterfly as he reacted to the shot, but the puck found a gap and tucked into the back of the net—score 1–0 Revolution on the short-handed goal. Kip raised his stick in celebration as he circled in behind the net. He was met by DJ on the other side.

"Way to go, Kipper," DJ praised his linemate.

The Raiders were frustrated by the goal against, but they shook it off and went to work as they tried to tie the game back up. McMahon's power-play unit remained on the ice and was able to gain control in the offensive zone. Newman and McMahon worked the puck low and tried to create a 2-on-1 with Matheson, once again. They pressured the young defender and were able to create some open space as they moved the puck.

McMahon drove the net after dropping the puck to Newman at the side of the net, but instead of returning the pass, Newman stepped out and took a shot on goal. Boushy stopped the shot, but he was unable to control the rebound. The puck bounced out into the slot, where it was met by McMahon as he entered the territory. McMahon continued with the puck as he averted his opponents and skated into open space to the right of Boushy. Pulling the goaltender further out toward him, McMahon slipped a nifty backdoor pass to Newman—tying the game at 1–1.

The Raiders gained back the momentum they had lost from the short-handed goal against, and built off the Newman strike. The Revolution could feel the ice tilt and they were on their heels as the second line came on for the Raiders. The line of Steven Frieberg, Riley Lamonte and Frankie Gallo was the hardest-working line for the team in black, and they were wearing out the Revolution defenders with a relentless attack. While the Revolution—and more specifically Edward Boushy—were able to fend off the pressure, the Raiders forced the goaltender to cover the puck and created an offensive faceoff for the upcoming line.

Coach Fitzgerald called upon Kole Kelley's line to enter into action as they defended their own zone. Flanking Kole were Mike McDennis and Joel Stevenson. The Raiders responded with a young line of their own, headed by Noah Mullen, who had led his Junior C team in scoring last season. The 18-year-old centre defeated Kole Kelley on the faceoff and won it back to his defence. Doug McCallister gained control on the blueline and inched his way across as McDennis approached. McCallister threw a knee-high wrist shot toward the goal and despite the traffic, the puck found its way past everyone—including Edward Boushy.

Out front, Andrew Boersman displayed his displeasure with the goal against and slammed Mullen to the ice as the Raider player instinctively celebrated the goal. An ensuing scrum commenced as tempers flared on both sides, but the referee only dished out the initial penalty to Boersman—resulting in another Raider power play. The McMahon unit once again returned to the ice to work on the man advantage.

McMahon won the draw at centre ice and the unit moved up the ice and gained control inside the Revolution zone. Newman skated the puck deeper into the zone, and buttonhooked on the half wall as he drew pressure from Donald Redman—escaping from the stick check. As he curled, he passed the puck up to the point. McCallister walked the line and drilled a slapshot toward the goal. Boushy met the blast with his right pad and kicked the puck back into the corner—where Newman regained control of the puck.

McMahon filtered in down low behind the net and provided an option for Newman, who impulsively passed the puck to his centre. Newman slid toward the post as he came out of the corner and received a quick return pass. Boushy dropped down as he anticipated the shot attempt, however, Newman fed a perfect seam pass up top to McCallister who was patrolling the area between the top of the circles. McCallister accepted the pass and slung a wrist shot toward the net as Boushy pushed back toward the centre of his net. The puck was labelled for the right side of the cage, but Boushy snagged it with his glove. McCallister looked up to the rafters in disbelief as he was robbed of his second goal of the period.

The period came to a close shortly after the unsuccessful Raiders' power play—keeping the score at 2–1 as the teams headed into the intermission. As the Revolution vacated the ice, they made sure to compliment their goalkeeper on his fabulous save; Boushy accepted their admiration humbly. It had been a relatively busy period for the goalie, having faced 15 shots against. The Revolution had managed nine shots toward Jeremy Vaux at the opposite end. They knew that a better effort would be needed as they entered the second period of play.

CHAPTER XVII

INTENSITY RISING

GM Bob Flaherty and Assistant GM Doug Chambers watched from high up in the stands. The two managers sat in anticipation of the second period, as both teams emerged onto the ice following the intermission. Brad Martinsen, who was still dealing with the side effects from the Kelley hit, joined the men.

"How are the headaches?" asked GM Flaherty.

"They come and go," replied Marty. "Every day is getting better, however, any sudden movements or overstraining of my neck really brings them on."

"You were just in for a re-evaluation, correct?" asked Assistant GM Chambers.

"Yes. I went in yesterday," said Marty. "They want me to work weekly with Dr. Andrews. They said he can help rehabilitate my neck muscles."

"What was the diagnosis?" questioned a concerned Assistant GM Chambers.

"Concussion and whiplash," replied Marty weakly. "No real timetable for when I can return to the ice, unfortunately."

"Yes, that is unfortunate," decreed GM Flaherty sincerely. "This will have an influence on how we proceed, I'm sad to say. I will still discuss the matter further with Coach Fitzgerald, so I don't want to alarm you…"

"I understand," responded Marty gloomily. "All I can do is try to work on myself. What happens outside of what I can control—I can't worry about."

"It is unsettling," said Assistant GM Chambers. "But I really admire your attitude, Brad. You are demonstrating maturity beyond your years!"

"I agree," stated GM Flaherty. "This is the kind of stuff—off the ice—that makes a big impression on coaching staff and management. Your play on the ice has a major impact, but we are always looking for complete players. We want players with leadership qualities and people that remain positive and uplifting."

"Thank you," said Marty with a smile.

Back on the ice, the Raiders had controlled most of the play as the second period moved along. By the halfway point, they led 3–1. A third goal had been scored by Frankie Gallo on a 2-on-1 rush. Spencer McIntyre was now warming up in the net, and he was set to begin the second half of the game. Edward Boushy had displayed some good goaltending during his time in net, however, he had let in three goals on 19 shots against.

Coach Fitzgerald used the brief break in action to address his team. "We need to pick it up out here, guys. This is the second game of the day for most of the Raiders' skaters—we need to push the pace. Get pucks deep. Get on their defence. Take the body and let them know you are there. You start to disrupt them in their own zone and you will create turnovers. We are down by two, but this game is not out of reach. Find it in yourselves to go out and make an impact on the ice!"

The Revolution rallied together as their coach's speech ended. The team had entered the break on a low, and to a man, they were re-entering on a high. It showed in their play as they immediately put pressure on the Raiders in the offensive zone. The line of Reinhart, Brown and Parker were able to hem the defence in their own zone and create some shots off turnovers—gaining an offensive zone faceoff for the Kelley line to start their shift on.

The top line came onto the ice and as they looked to capitalize on the faceoff, Kip aligned his wingers and defence accordingly. Kip leaned in for the draw and defeated his opposition swiftly—pulling the puck back to Curtis Kraemer. Kraemer made a quick pass along the blueline to Victor Sharp, who lined up in the middle of the ice. As Sharp gained control of the puck, his time and space were invaded by the oncoming defender, forcing the Revolution defender to direct the puck toward the goal off target.

Trent Rosenberg manned the front of the net and watched the shot come toward the slot. He swung his stick at the puck as it sailed by and redirected the shot on goal. The quick change in direction caught Jeremy Vaux by surprise, but the 6'3" goaltender used his quick reflexes to kick out the attempt with his left pad. The puck dribbled off to where the faceoff had taken place.

The two centres began a loose puck battle—with Kip coming away with it through his vigorous effort. Kip protected the puck from the defender with his body, as he skated low into the zone. DJ found himself high in the zone and began to float into the empty space on the weak side of the ice as Rosenberg garnered the attention out front of the net.

"Kipper!" shouted DJ as he snuck in on the backside of the goal. Kip continued to shield the puck as the opposing player fought desperately to knock him off it. He heard DJ's cry for the puck and could see him through the crowd in front. Knowing a direct pass could be easily intercepted, Kip banked a pass off the end boards and allowed his winger to take over control.

DJ picked up the puck and pivoted to scope his options. With his fellow linemates well covered, he scanned his secondary choices and spotted Victor Sharp. Sharp had moved to the top of the circle just above the faceoff dot; he called for a pass and DJ sent it out rapidly. The pass connected with a one-time slapshot that whistled in on the Raiders' net. Jeremy Vaux tracked the play well and was equal to the task once again—dropping into the butterfly and swallowing up the puck as it hit his body. DJ moved out from behind the net and searched for a rebound, however, he was plowed over with a stiff cross-check by the Raiders' Dustin MacDonald.

MacDonald stood overtop of DJ and snarled, "What? You gonna do something?"

"Whatever, buddy!" responded DJ timidly. "Nice cross-check!"

"You liked that?" questioned MacDonald, as he bent over to give him another one on the ice. Kip Kelley charged in to defend his young winger and tackled MacDonald to the ice. Kip and MacDonald tussled on the ice as the rest of the players formed a scrum in front of the Raiders' goal. The referees and linesmen got in quickly to break up the skirmish and then proceeded to hand out penalties.

"You better keep your head up, Kelley!" yelled MacDonald as the two were separated by the linesmen. "Next shift, we're going!"

Kelley laughed at the remark. "You're not worth my time, man! We'll send out Northgate after you, dude! Just wait."

The two players were ushered to their respective penalty boxes and given roughing penalties—Frankie Gallo joined them to serve the initial cross-checking penalty. DJ, Rosenberg, Sharp and Kraemer remained on the ice and were joined by Kole Kelley to start the power play. Kole would look to take advantage of the opportunity to showcase his skills as he moved into his brother's role.

On the faceoff, Kole was able to tie up the Raiders' centreman, allowing DJ to charge in and poke the puck back to Kraemer. As the Revolution gained control to start, the players shifted into their power play formation as they fended off the aggressive defensive pressure early. The power-play unit moved the puck around smartly to settle down the penalty killers and then looked to set up for a goal.

Kole Kelley took control of the puck as DJ moved it down low to him. DJ skated hard toward the net and looked for a return pass, but Kole looked him off and skated up to where DJ had been positioned previously. The defenders inched down toward the goal as DJ pressed in, which allowed Rosenberg to take a step back and away from coverage. Kole saw the play unfold and sent a quick pass into Rosenberg—who snapped the puck past the blocker on the far side of the goal. The Revolution now trailed by one.

The team looked to build off the power-play goal and continued to pressure the Raiders. Turcotte's line followed up with a few good scoring chances on the next shift, but Jeremy Vaux bounced back immediately and was standing tall in goal, stopping every shot resulting from persistent attack. The Revolution's third and fourth lines were determined to tie the game back up, but the ample number of attempts were all deterred.

"Let's tie this baby up!" shouted Kip as he rejoined his linemates on the ice after serving his penalty. The Kelley line positioned themselves for the neutral zone faceoff against McMahon and his wingers.

"DJ!" screeched Coach Fitzgerald as he waved his player to the bench. Coming over the boards was James Northgate. Coach Fitzgerald realized that MacDonald was back on the ice for the Raiders. DJ skated off the ice and was relieved by Northgate at the left-wing position. The puck was dropped and play resumed with Northgate overseeing the Revolution's top stars.

They were able to get the puck in deep and Northgate skated in while watching as MacDonald went back for the puck in the corner. Seeing an opportunity to make a bodycheck, the big-bodied winger drove in hard and laid out the Raiders' defenceman as he rimmed the puck around the glass.

"Do we have a problem?" asked Northgate as he looked down at MacDonald on the ice. MacDonald didn't respond to the skater standing overtop of him and got up in a bit of pain. Northgate began to skate away, but the Raiders' defender had other plans—*WHACK!* MacDonald laid a two-handed slash across the forearm of the winger in retaliation.

Northgate screeched in anguish and turned around to face his opponent. "Are we doing this then?" The two players tangled up and began to scuffle. The 6'4" Revolution forward had the height and reach advantage over his adversary and used it to get the best of MacDonald. The linesmen weren't far behind the beginning of the fight and made sure they divided the players up effectively once Northgate took MacDonald to the ice.

Players from both sides huddled around the scene and showed their approval of their teammates' efforts—tapping their sticks on the ice as the two skaters were escorted off the ice to go to the dressing rooms.

"DJ, get back out there!" hollered Coach Fitzgerald. As DJ lined up for the neutral zone faceoff, he received a nasty cross-check to the side of his ribs.

"Babysitter's gone, buddy!" said Tyler Jacobs nastily. Jacobs was a rugged right winger and played a physical game. "You going to man up?"

DJ gave him a cross-check back, but he was pushed aside by Andrew Boersman who was playing behind the Kelley line on defence.

"Are you looking for somebody to dance with?" Boersman questioned heatedly.

"This kid can't defend himself?" Jacobs laughed.

"He's out here to bury you on the scoreboard," Boersman fired back. "Touch him and you've got the rest of us to deal with."

Boersman and Jacob's verbal sparring escalated into a shoving match before they were separated. The refs issued both players game misconducts as they tried to relieve some of the intensity building between the two teams. After the penalties were handed out, the refs split up to talk to both coaches.

"Back to hockey, Coach," said the referee visiting the Revolution bench. "Any more of these scrums and we're going to keep tossing out players, or we'll only be taking one side to the box. Got it?"

"Understood," replied Coach Fitzgerald respectfully.

In the dying minutes of the period, both teams got back to playing hockey and provided some end-to-end action. Neither team was able to tally another strike, so the score remained 3–2 as they left the ice for the second intermission.

Coach Fitzgerald crossed the ice and entered the room behind his players. "Great effort in the last ten minutes out there guys! We played hard. We played as a team. We looked out for one another!" He paused and looked around at his team proudly. "Those are the things that bring us closer together! Let's keep up the good work when we get back out there. We've got this!"

CHAPTER XVIII

TO THE FINISH

The third period picked up right where the last period ended as both teams looked to capture the next goal. The Revolution and the Raiders knew that the sixth goal of the game—if scored—would be a crucial one in determining the outcome. For the Revolution, it meant they would have battled back and drawn even. With it would come added momentum as they would pursue the go-ahead goal to finish off the third period. On the other side, the Raiders knew that restoring a two-goal lead could stunt the push their opponents were making and maybe create the separation they needed to win the game.

The teams traded chances, but both Spencer McIntyre and Jeremy Vaux defended their nets strongly as they went toe to toe in the save department. On top of the spectacular goaltending, the offensive prowess both teams possessed continued to break through and put pressure on the defensive systems the opposition provided. More specifically, the Kelley line for the Revolution and the McMahon line for the Raiders looked extremely dangerous and threatened to score the all-important next goal of the game. The two lines found themselves facing the hand-picked checking line from the opposing coaches, but neither side seemed to have the ability to shut them down as they both tried to limit scoring opportunities.

The first quarter of the period had ticked away and the McMahon line came on for their third shift of the period. Coach Fitzgerald called upon the Kelley line to go head-to-head with them as the team changed on-the-fly.

"Kip!" called out Coach Fitzgerald. "Go make them play in their own end!"

"Aye aye," responded Kip eagerly.

The trio of Kip, DJ and Rosenberg made their way onto the ice and were able to provide a shift in momentum as they turned over the puck in the neutral zone. Rosenberg flipped the puck high into the corner and DJ raced in to try to pick up the loose puck. As he got into the corner, DJ felt the pressure from the defender on his right shoulder and chipped the puck back behind the goal before absorbing a hard check into the boards.

Kip followed the puck down deep and gained control of it. Greg McMahon trailed in behind him and ensured that a lane to the net would be well defended. Kip protected the puck as he skated around the perimeter up to the half wall. His options were limited, so he spun and ripped the puck back into the corner—calculating one of his wingers to be roaming in the area. His prediction was correct and Rosenberg dropped into the corner from out front of the net and retained possession for the Revolution.

DJ called for the puck to return to him in the opposite corner, as he remained positioned there following the check he had endured. Rosenberg banked a pass to DJ and started toward the net. Kip had circled into the middle and had already begun a net drive as he watched his linemates move the puck to the weak side of the ice. DJ took control of the puck and drew the attention of the defence once again. As the defender pressed in on him, DJ shifted to the left and then jumped back to the right—pulling the puck between the legs of the oncoming player. The move worked perfectly and he found himself with an uncontested lane to the net.

"DJ!" screeched Kip as he broke away from McMahon on defence. DJ saw Kip had a step on his check and sent a pass to the slot. Kip met the pass in stride and he flawlessly directed the puck to Rosenberg on the backside of the goal. Rosenberg made no mistake as he caressed the pass and jammed it into the empty cage—making it a 3–3 hockey game. The Revolution's bench erupted into cheers as they witnessed the puck enter the net. The skaters on the ice did a flyby of the bench and then went down to tap McIntyre on the pad before returning to the faceoff circle.

"Way to go, boys!" announced Coach Fitzgerald as he worked up and down the bench. "Let's keep going! Don't take your foot off the throttle!"

The game continued and the Revolution looked to build off their gained energy, but the Raiders were able to hold their form from the drop of the puck. The back-and-forth action continued beyond the halfway point of the period, with neither team able to get the upper hand on the scoreboard. Eventually, the Raiders' coach utilized an offensive zone faceoff to gain a favourable matchup. He implemented the McMahon line against the line of Reinhart, Brown and Parker, after the Revolution's line had iced the puck unintentionally on an erred pass.

McMahon squared up with Reinhart on the faceoff and managed to kick the puck back to Miles Newman on the boards. Newman darted across the top of the circle and threw a quick wrist shot toward the net, but Spencer

McIntyre had no difficulty in deflecting the shot into the far corner. The Raiders were quick to the rebound as Ryder Parrish picked it up in the corner and circled up toward the blueline. Anson Brown tried to close off his lane, but Parrish chipped the puck off the wall to Doug McCallister on the point. Knowing he was drawn out of position, Brown made sure to finish his check on Parrish.

McCallister gathered up the puck and wound up to take a shot on goal, however, he faked the shot as Reinhart dropped down to block the shot in front of him. With the Revolution centre down, McCallister stickhandled the puck around him and closed in toward the goal. As he approached the top of the circle, he sent a quick wrist shot toward the traffic gathered in front of the net. McMahon freed up his stick and deflected the puck up toward the top corner of the goal. McIntyre stuck out his glove and robbed McMahon of the go-ahead tally.

In the corner, Brown began to skate away from the check he had made, but suffered a slash to the back of his leg. Without hesitation, he whirled around and shoved Parrish backwards. The push sent the Raiders' winger off balance and down on the ice.

TWEET…

"White… two minutes for roughing after the whistle!" shouted the official.

"Are you kidding me?" sounded a baffled Anson Brown. "He just hacked me in the leg!"

"Get to the box," declared the referee.

The penalty came with just under seven minutes remaining in the period and left the Revolution with a difficult task. Coach Fitzgerald tapped Kip and DJ on the shoulders to start the kill.

"Don't hesitate to jump on any opportunity up ice," said Kip as the two forwards skated out for the faceoff. "Look to fly the zone if I win this draw!"

"Sounds good," replied DJ.

On the faceoff, Kip was successful and won the puck back to the corner. Kraemer had to be quick, but he managed to launch the puck high above the heads of all the Raiders and clear the defensive zone. DJ was on his toes off the draw and did exactly as Kip had instructed him to do. He watched Kraemer as he shot the puck and sped out toward the neutral zone. DJ wasn't able to track the puck as he focused on the defenders in front of him, but he anticipated the puck would land somewhere beyond the redline.

Doug McCallister backtracked and seemed to have an eye on the puck, so DJ expected the puck to land near the Raiders' captain. Suddenly, the puck entered into his sight. McCallister reached up with his glove to take control, however, he was unable to maintain possession as it came down and skipped in behind him. DJ pushed up the ice and poked the puck away from McCallister. The defender was caught standing still and DJ zoomed off toward the Raiders' zone with the puck.

DJ had a clear lane to the goal, but he knew that he had the other defender hot on his heels. He closed in on Jeremy Vaux in net and examined his options quickly. He noticed Vaux playing out pretty far from his crease, so he decided that faking a shot and deking would be his best option. As he closed in, he positioned himself to shoot—lifting his weak-side leg as part of his deception. The trickery worked and Vaux bit on the fake, slightly sinking into a save. At that moment, DJ pulled the puck to his backhand—which further fooled the goaltender into dropping into action—and then quickly back to his forehand. The move had completely buckled Jeremy Vaux and left nearly half of the net to shoot into, but as DJ went to bury the puck, his stick was lifted and he was stripped of the opportunity.

The hard backcheck from Gregory Wild prevented the Revolution from scoring their second short-handed goal of the game and sent the action back toward the other end of the ice. DJ could not believe his luck, but he had no time to languish as he had to get back to help defensively. The Raiders pressed hard on their return to the offensive zone, but the defence held strong and killed off the remaining portion of Brown's penalty.

"Great try, guys!" stated Coach Fitzgerald as he knelt down behind DJ and Kip and placed a hand on each of their shoulders.

"Thanks, Coach!" replied DJ and Kip simultaneously.

"Man, I can't believe he broke that up!" declared Kip as the coach moved away.

"Unbelievable, right?" replied a frustrated DJ. "I should have just shot."

"You had him down and out," responded Kip enthusiastically. "You made the right play. It was just an incredible effort by their player."

"Yeah, I guess," said DJ half-heartedly.

The two watched the play from the bench, knowing that they might get one or two shifts before the third period was over. With under four minutes left to go, Turcotte's line broke out of their own end and moved down the ice. Turcotte held onto the puck as he entered the offensive zone and gave a quick drop pass to Harrison Gage who trailed in behind him. Joel Stevenson, who was filling in James Northgate's spot following his ejection from the game, was busting hard to the net.

"Shoot!" boomed Coach Fitzgerald from the bench.

Whether Gage heard the coach or had come to the decision on his own, he shot a quick, hard wrist shot at Jeremy Vaux. Dozer continued hard toward the goaltender, and Vaux was aware of the oncoming skater. The goaltender made a pad save and deflected the rebound out beyond Dozer's reach in the slot.

The smooth-skating Martin Killington was fresh off the bench as the play headed toward the Raiders' zone and utilized his speed to turn it into a four-man attack. As Vaux poked the puck away from Stevenson, Killington quickly raced in and gathered up the loose puck. Finding himself free from immediate pressure, he lifted his head and saw that Vaux had moved out to challenge him on a rebound attempt. Killington made sure to keep his feet moving as he pulled the puck onto his forehand and looked to skate around the goalie. Vaux made an effort to stay with the defenceman as he moved laterally, but Killington's quickness opened up a hole to the right of the goaltender and he shot the puck to the back of the net to bring the game to 4–3 for the Revolution.

"Whoo!" screamed Dozer as he scooped up Killington in the corner to celebrate the goal. The five Revolution skaters broke out of their huddle in the corner and returned for a round of high-fives at the bench.

"Awesome goal!" Coach Fitzgerald proclaimed as the players came onto the bench. "Alright guys, we have 3:17 left to play. We need to get pucks out and we need to get pucks in deep. Make them come through all five skaters— no turnovers!"

The referee blew his whistle to instruct the Revolution to hurry up for the faceoff at centre ice. Kole Kelley and his line jumped over the boards and went out to try to defend the lead. The line was effective and managed to burn off another 42 seconds. They were followed by the Reinhart line who were also able to kill roughly another minute.

With the clock sitting at 1:25, the Raiders sent the McMahon line to the ice; the Revolution responded with Kip Kelley's line. Initially, the Raiders had a difficult time trying to advance the puck into the offensive zone, but as play entered into the last 40 seconds of the game, a quick transition up to Miles Newman allowed them to do so. Newman had few options and opted to throw a shot on net from the perimeter—the puck was easily contained by Spencer McIntyre. McMahon and Parrish barged in on goal, which forced McIntyre to hold on for the whistle.

The teams lined up for the faceoff in the defensive zone, however, Captain Doug McCallister skated over to the referee and motioned for a Raiders' time out. Both sides returned to their respective benches for instruction—and more importantly some rest—as the two teams looked to keep their top lines on the ice to finish the game. Coach Fitzgerald gave a few instructions on how he wanted the players to line up and what to do on a won draw or lost draw, but overall he remained calm and collected and expressed confidence in his players. The buzzer sounded to alert both teams to the fact that the 30-second timeout was complete, and everyone returned to the Revolution's zone for the faceoff. Jeremy Vaux stayed on the Raiders' bench and was replaced by an extra attacker.

Kip moved in against McMahon as the star players set to battle for control. The linesman threw the puck to the ice and the centres clashed their sticks together. The puck remained close as they battled and the wingers were left with the mission of retrieving the puck and gaining possession for their team. DJ charged in shoulder to shoulder with Ryder Parrish. Parrish gave DJ a stern bump and knocked him away to gain control for the Raiders before sending a pass back to McCallister at the blueline.

McCallister received the puck and looked to make a play toward the net. Trent Rosenberg had effectively taken away a lane to the net, so McCallister passed the puck cross-ice to Gregory Wild. Taking possession of the puck, Wild delivered a quick pass down to Miles Newman in the corner. Newman's creative mind had already been on display throughout the game and he looked to deliver once again. He stickhandled back toward the half wall and examined his options. Greg McMahon slid in behind the net to support his winger and Newman cycled the puck back down below the goal line to him.

Taking control of the puck down low, the right-handed McMahon turned out quickly and aggressively attempted to drive to the front of the net. He was met physically by Donald Redman, but still managed to jam the puck on net. McIntyre held his post and stopped the puck with his pad; the rebound shot out to the right and Miles Newman regained control of it. Newman attempted to snipe a shot over the shoulder of McIntyre. The shot whistled by the goaltender's ear—*TING!*

The puck blasted off the crossbar and ricocheted off to the far boards. DJ followed the puck with his eyes and skated over to it as it bounced off the side wall. He picked it up and in one motion he lobbed the puck high off the glass, over McCallister's head and into the neutral zone. Gregory Wild urgently skated back to get the puck. Wild whipped back around and toward the Revolution's end, but it was too late. The buzzer sounded to end the game.

The Revolution had scored three unanswered goals to erase a 3–1 deficit and win the game. They would advance to tomorrow's game to play for third overall. The players got up from the bench and celebrated with Spencer McIntyre at the Revolution's net.

"Great game, Spence!" said DJ proudly and tapped his goaltender on the helmet. "You were a wall back here today."

"Thanks, DJ," McIntyre replied happily. "You had a good game, too!"

The Revolution vacated the ice and returned to their dressing room. Coach Fitzgerald came in and congratulated the team on the victory.

"Great come-from-behind win, gentlemen! We accomplished our goal and will play for third place tomorrow. Before leaving, I would like the following players to meet with us in the stands: Spencer McIntyre; Edward Boushy; Victor Sharp; Eric Matheson; Andrew Boersman; Martin Killington; Kole Kelley; Mike McDennis; Anson Brown; Steve Reinhart; Scott Parker; and DJ Roberts. I will see the rest of you tomorrow!"

CHAPTER XIX

NARROWING DOWN THE ROSTER

In the stands, the Revolution staff were deep in discussion as they tried to narrow down the roster before heading into the big matchup. The next day's game with either the Jaguars or the Bandits would be their last chance to look at players before finalizing the roster, and it would be their last game heading into opening weekend of the coming season. The staff needed to evaluate the talent vying for a spot with the team and see how players would handle themselves in game situations. The staff came up with a list of players that they felt they could sign and a list of players they could part ways with. While several players were easy to settle on, others created conflict in the conversation.

"So, we'd like to sign Reinhart, Boersman and Killington on the spot," GM Flaherty summarized. "Our list of definite releases includes Boushy, MacKenzie, Norris and Manson. We are still debating which direction to go with Kole Kelley, Brown, Parker and Ryerson, and we have to decide what to do with our underage cards, including Brad Martinsen. Do we agree with this?"

"Yes… I'd say that's where we stand," replied Coach Fitzgerald.

"Alright," said GM Flaherty. "I, for one, feel confident with the four players in question. Kole has shown he is quite capable of filling a depth role and can provide some secondary scoring. Brown has displayed some good qualities and adds some grit to the bottom six. If we are pushing out both Norris and Manson, then Brown is the reason and that should merit him a spot. Parker has incredible speed and can utilize it to be a game-breaker—short-handed or on transition. He can be outmatched physically, but he is feisty and is never hesitant to engage into action. Lastly, Ryerson adds some depth and brings mobility on the back end. He doesn't shy away from the physical side of the game. We are also light on defence and he has the potential to blossom under some quality leadership."

"I can't argue with your analysis," responded Coach Fitzgerald. "They all deserve a chance for at least one final showing tomorrow."

"What are we going to do with our underage cards?" said Assistant GM Chambers eagerly. "We have a great selection, and it will play a pivotal role in how some of these other skaters' fates will fall."

"DJ?" GM Flaherty threw out the name of the biggest impact player in the mix for an underage position.

"I want him!" replied Coach Fitzgerald confidently. "He has shown me everything I have wanted and expected of him. He has earned the right to play amongst our best players and it is only fair that he knows heading into the game tomorrow that he has his place on the team."

"Then what?" asked Assistant GM Chambers. "We have Burrow, McDennis, Sharp and Matheson showing us why they belong. Not to mention Martinsen, who may only be out for a little bit to start the year."

"That's a dilemma," stated GM Flaherty. "I personally feel that Brad Martinsen represents the highest quality of these players."

"That doesn't always account for everything," Coach Fitzgerald responded sharply. "We have skill up front, but our back end is shallow."

"Sharp has the ability to play at this level," piped up Assistant Coach McIntosh. "He has been strong all camp long."

"You want to risk losing Marty to some other team?" responded GM Flaherty bluntly. "The season is 54 games long—I am comfortable letting him work his way back into the lineup if it means we are a better team as the season moves along. I will find other defencemen."

"How bloated are we looking to be up front?" questioned Coach Fitzgerald. "With all due respect to the kid, I have Turcotte and Cooke playing behind Kip and could very well have Kole as well. Our wings are solid too! Where do guys go if we continue to inflate our lineup up front? I can't imagine guys will be too thrilled if they get pushed down—or out of the lineup."

"I know I don't have to explain this to you," GM Flaherty started, "but this is junior hockey, Fitzy. It's not about whether guys like where they stand in the lineup, it is about showing you deserve to be where you are! When you have a player that has outperformed others, you can't shun him off because he suffered an injury—that's my opinion. Martinsen was hands down the best skater on the ice prior to that hit. I don't think you can deny that?"

"Yes," agreed Coach Fitzgerald, "he was an impact player. But his return is up in the air! What if his symptoms continue long-term? When I have other skaters that could help the team, I can't rest on my laurels and disregard the potential fact of Brad Martinsen not playing—or even not playing to that level—again this season."

"Okay, let's take Martinsen out of the equation temporarily," announced Assistant GM Chambers. "Is Sharp the best option? I honestly have been captivated by Brendan Burrow. He is a big centre and we aren't big up the middle. He has had immediate chemistry with Roberts. We talk about losing Martinsen, but I can't imagine that this guy hasn't made an impression on anyone else who watched him against the Hawks. He is as steady as steady can be!"

"He has been a favourite of mine," concurred Coach Fitzgerald. "Steady is correct! I want to see him again tomorrow. For me, it is between him and Sharp for this second spot—if we do sign a second underage card."

"I agree. It's tough to argue against Burrow and what he has shown," added GM Flaherty. "He plays a two-way game and engages himself on every shift."

"Going forward, whoever doesn't sign deserves to affiliate with us," stated Assistant Coach Horton. "Assuming they don't sign with another team."

"That's right," said Coach Fitzgerald in agreeance. "Bob, what are the chances that Martinsen is good with playing another season of AAA or going to a Junior B or C team so we can use him that way?"

"Hmm… it's something we can discuss with him, I suppose…" replied GM Flaherty half-heartedly. "I think it's a mistake to leave him available though."

"Either way we slice this, Bob," responded Coach Fitzgerald sharply, "we are exposing a good player to another team. I get that you may have a personal relationship with him, but I have doubts on what he may be capable of going forward if this injury is as severe as it sounds."

"I understand," said GM Flaherty. "But don't assume my position on him has anything to do with my relationship with him outside of the game. He has earned my vote based on what he is capable of on the ice and what he would bring to the team off the ice as well."

"McDennis and Matheson are chopped liver then?" questioned Assistant GM Chambers.

"McDennis has played really well, but that right side is jammed," said Coach Fitzgerald.

"He doesn't beat out the others in the underage card race," added GM Flaherty. "I do believe he is more apt to stay local and play another year of midget or catch on with a Junior B or C team. He will likely be willing to affiliate."

"Yes," granted Coach Fitzgerald. "As for Matheson, I want to see him again. He has been behind Sharp thus far, but he could possibly unseat him tomorrow. There hasn't been that much separation between the two."

Shortly after the discussion, the players started to come up—one-by-one—to pay a visit to the staff and learn their standing with the team. The staff discussed with each Revolution hopeful what they saw in their game that they liked, and what they felt they could work on. Unfortunately for a few of the players, their journey would end. For each individual that was parting ways, the staff tried to ensure that they left with a positive outlook on their experience and with optimism as they continued on their own hockey path.

DJ was mixed in the middle of the group of players waiting to talk to the staff. He waited patiently as he watched the action between the Jaguars and Bandits out on the ice, and he started to feel a bit uneasy as his heart rate increased in anticipation. He felt his legs begin to bounce and twiddled his fingers as he mentally prepared for his meeting. He was confident in himself and his game, however, not knowing his destiny was extremely nerve-racking for the young forward. Finally, he was waved over to meet with the staff.

"Great game out there," GM Flaherty said as he greeted the left-winger. "Have a seat."

"Thanks," replied DJ.

"Well, DJ," said Coach Fitzgerald. "You rebounded today with a great effort, and I was really excited to see that. You've worked hard all camp and have been one of the top performers. Having said that… we would like to officially offer you a position with the Revolution!"

"Wow!" DJ said. He was pleasantly surprised. Even with his level of self-confidence, he was humbled by Coach Fitzgerald's straight-forwardness. "This is incredible. Thank you!"

"I know we kind of strung you along," Coach Fitzgerald continued, "but you were always in our minds as being a lock. We wanted to see how you would respond to a prolonged process, and you did so admirably."

"Thank you," replied DJ. "I look forward to representing the Revolution!"

"And you will be back in the lineup tomorrow," said Coach Fitzgerald. "Same line! Go out there and cement your spot at the top!" Coach Fitzgerald took a quick glance at the scoreboard. "Looks like we will be facing the Bandits!"

CHAPTER XX

GM#3 > REVOLUTION VS BANDITS

The Raiders and Black Knights were in the midst of the action as DJ walked into the arena to prepare for their game against the Bandits. The Bandits had eventually lost to the Jaguars the night before—losing by a score of 7–2. It had been the Bandits' second game of the day, and it had been a quick turnaround after their win over the Black Knights in the afternoon. Regardless, the Bandits were no match for the high-powered Jags who had dropped them to the second-tier matchup on Sunday with the Revolution. DJ took a moment to watch the game before carrying on down to the team's dressing room. The Raiders were off to a good start and were leading 3–1 as the first period came to a close.

As DJ picked up his bag and sticks and walked toward the room he heard someone holler at him from the lobby.

"Hey, DJ!" It was Marty, who was just on his way in. "Awesome game yesterday, buddy!"

"Marty!" greeted DJ happily. The two bumped fists as they came together. "How are you feeling?"

"Better each day, thankfully!" announced Marty with a modest smile. "Hoping I'm not too far off a return to the ice."

"Man! That would be great!" declared DJ. "What's the vibe from the team?"

"Uncertain," said Marty. "Bob and his assistant were very courteous when I gave them the update, but it still had to go through everyone. So…"

"The unknown!" said DJ. "Well, I have faith that whatever is best for you will happen. You deserve to be here."

"Thanks," responded Marty graciously. "I just hope that there are no setbacks and I can get back into rhythm. It's such a big year for us! I don't want to miss out on anything because of this."

DJ nodded in agreement and they stood in silence and digested the topic.

"What's the word with you? Signed yet?"

DJ laughed as his friend turned the subject back on him. "Yes, after the game yesterday. It was a relief to get it out of the way."

"Oh… that is fantastic," responded Marty. "I'm so happy for you, dude!"

"Thanks!"

"Well, I won't hold you up from going to get ready. Good luck out there!"

"Talk to you later, buddy."

DJ continued down the hallway to the Revolution's dressing room. He was happy Marty had caught him before he had gone in to get ready for the game. Marty had been such a positive influence on him over the years and always inspired DJ to be a better player and—more importantly—a better human being.

As he approached the room, he realized Coach Fitzgerald had posted the lineup on the outside of the door. Just as indicated in the talk yesterday, he found himself alongside Kip Kelley and Trent Rosenberg. He also saw that the team would have the veteran presence of Carter Riddle in net, as well as both Wallace Black and Dallas Freeman on the back end. He knew that this lineup would closely resemble the one that would carry into next weekend, with a few adjustments. The presence of some of these key pieces was very uplifting and DJ was extremely proud to be part of the Revolution today.

<u>GM#3 vs The Bandits</u>

DJ Roberts – Kip Kelley – Trent Rosenberg
Harrison Gage – JJ Turcotte – James Northgate
Stewart Cooke – Brendan Burrow – Kole Kelley
Anson Brown – Steve Reinhart – Scott Parker

Wallace Black – Dallas Freeman
Victor Sharp – Donald Redman
Eric Matheson – Cody Ryerson

Carter Riddle
Spencer McIntyre

Everyone was focused as they physically and mentally prepared for the upcoming matchup. Coach Fitzgerald and his assistants were hovering around the area and involved in some small talk and going over minor details with various individuals around the room. As time progressed, Coach Fitzgerald took a moment to address the team as a whole.

"Alright, guys!" Coach Fitzgerald garnered the attention of the skaters. "If you told me that we could be playing for third overall in this tournament before it began, I would take it. We knew we had some tough competition in the Hawks and Raiders during the round robin—and we knew that we were coming in here without any prior history of playing together. That is a factor we have overcome, and now we have the ability to walk away from this tournament and head into the regular season on a high note. We can come away from here today with a win over a team that finished fifth overall last season and advanced to the second round of the playoffs. And while it may not seem like this is the time of year to be overly ecstatic about a win like this, we are not in the same position as other teams are. Everything we accomplish this season needs to be on a positive learning curve! Friday night's loss and yesterday's win were both experiences in which we learned about ourselves—what we have and what we don't have. Tonight, let's show the Bandits that when you step on the ice with the Revolution, you're stepping into a dogfight! Be relentless. Be persistent. Go out and show them that the Revolution has arrived… and we are going to make an impact!"

The team consumed their coach's speech, and were captivated by his words. The energy was running rampant as Assistant Coach McIntosh came in to announce that the ice was ready. The veterans on the team were vocal as they led the team to the warm-up—evidence that the team was beginning to unite.

"Here we go!" shouted Kip Kelley. "It's our time, guys!"

"Fire it up here in warmies!" yelled Wallace Black. "They aren't going to touch us tonight!"

The team made their way out for warm-up and were flying as they took to the ice. Their passes were crisp and on point, and their shots were like missiles as they left the blades of their sticks. The players were ready to go!

The opening faceoff was moments away and the two teams heard their final directions and headed out to lineup for the puck drop. DJ, Kip and Rosenberg came together before taking their position for the draw.

"Alright, it's show time, boys!" announced Kip. "Build off of what we accomplished together yesterday and we'll be doing alright for ourselves. DJ, you keep grinding it out and winning the board battles like you are. Rosie—well, you know where to find those gaps. We'll do our best to get you some looks."

"You won't regret it," Rosenberg laughed confidently.

"I know I won't." Kip grinned.

DJ laughed along with his teammates, but he wondered if they were overlooking their opponent's abilities slightly. He felt uncomfortable voicing his concerns, so he turned his attention back to what he could control—his game. He knew the game ahead would be difficult and he was ready to put in the work needed to help his team achieve success. The players broke away to their positions. The referee motioned to both goaltenders to ensure they were ready to go, and just like that, the battle for third began.

Kip Kelley and Kirby Rollins dug in as they fought for the opening possession of the game. Kip and Rollins engaged physically, but Rollins was able to twist his body and he kicked the puck back to his defenceman.

The Bandits controlled the puck and patiently awaited the attack from the Revolution. DJ broke through and put some pressure on the Bandits' captain, Ryan O'Rourke. The big defenceman easily bypassed the oncoming pursuit as he relayed the puck to his partner. Lucas Danielsson received the puck and looked up the ice. Rollins was in a pocket between the forechecking line and the defenders and provided an easy target for his defenceman. Danielsson blasted the puck in his direction and Rollins redirected it in behind the veteran tandem of Dallas Freeman and Wallace Black.

Black had anticipated the pass and stepped up on the top scorer for the Bandits and landed a punishing hit. The player on the bench went wild in admiration of Black's hit, but the referee disagreed and deemed the hit to be late.

TWEET...

"Two minutes for interference!" shouted the ref as he pointed toward the towering defenceman.

Black shook his head in disgust, but quietly skated to the box to serve his penalty.

The Bandits removed Danielsson from the ice and replaced him with their top goal scorer from last season, Nick Peters. On the opposite side, the Revolution called Rosenberg off and added Donald Redman to replace Black on the backend.

The puck dropped and Kip won it cleanly back to Freeman—who controlled it and fired it hard around the boards. The Bandits couldn't keep it from clearing the zone, so they started a breakout from their own zone.

They curled back and turned up ice in a five-man unit. Rollins possessed the puck and brought it back up through the middle of the ice. DJ defended the middle of the ice as he approached the blueline and tried to force a turnover as Rollins approached. The skillful centreman placed an effortless pass to Peters, who was streaking up the right side of the ice.

Peters took the pass and broke in over the redline and into the offensive zone. He felt some pressure from Kip over his shoulder and knew that Freeman had taken away his ability to skate deeper into the zone without risking a turnover. Peters stopped hard in his tracks, spun out toward the boards and opened up to pass the puck to his supporting power-play members.

Rollins positioned himself on the point and gave a quick wave with his stick to notify his teammate he was ready for the pass. Peters sent the puck accordingly. As he cradled the incoming puck, Rollins scanned the surrounding ice and continued to move the puck across to the left side of the ice as he dished it to his captain on the opposite point.

O'Rourke pulled the puck across his body and wound up for a slapshot, however, he was testing the oncoming defender to see if he could pull him down and out of position. DJ was in his path and did his best to take away the shooting lane without having to overcommit on a block. O'Rourke controlled the puck and sent a return pass to Rollins on his right side.

Rollins took control in motion as he moved toward the centre of the ice. This opened up a quick seam pass to Geoff Altoy who had found a home off to the right side of Riddle in net. The big right winger didn't waste any time in making a play toward the net and powered his way from the goal line and tried to jam the puck behind Riddle.

Riddle dropped down and maintained strong positioning and fought hard to keep the puck out of the net. After a few good whacks, the whistle sounded and brought the play to an end.

"Good job, Carter!" announced Kip as he circled in to give his goalie a tap on the pads.

All nine players remained on the ice for the following faceoff and Kip lined up against Rollins once more. Kip won the draw for another quick clearing attempt by Dallas Freeman. Freeman did indeed clear the puck once again and the penalty-killing forwards were called to the bench for a change.

"Great job on those faceoff wins, Kipper," exclaimed his teammates and coaches as he climbed onto the bench.

Replacing them on the ice were Steve Reinhart and Scott Parker. Both tried to apply some pressure up ice to prohibit the power play from advancing, however, the slick puck handling from Rollins was too much and he was able to enter the offensive zone uncontested.

"More pressure!" was the order from the Revolution bench.

However, the direction from the coaching staff proved to be ineffective as the Bandits zipped the puck around the perimeter and limited the amount of pressure they received. The puck found its way back to Rollins who was working from the top of the zone. He pulled in Reinhart as he gained control and sent a quick pass to Peters. Peters played give-and-go with Altoy in the right corner before returning a pass up top to Rollins.

Rollins was in a great position to one-time the pass and lifted his stick as he timed the oncoming puck. Scott Parker tracked the puck perfectly and dropped down in front of the shot, however, the puck was one-touched hard back toward Peters. As it got to him, Peters hammered the puck with a one-timer of his own and the puck sailed hard and high over the shoulder of Riddle—score 1–0 Bandits!

The Bandits' bench and their few fans in attendance erupted in celebration of the opening goal—which occurred only 1:18 into the game. Black returned to the ice and skated over to the bench with his head down.

"Shake it off!" shouted Kip cheerfully. "You're fine, Blacky! Tough call, bud!"

As a whole, the Revolution were able to shake off the unfortunate start and gain some traction with some good 5-on-5 shifts following the power-play goal against. The play was upbeat and both teams were able to generate some good opportunities, however, both goaltenders held their ground and kept the score 1–0 as the first period came to a close with the Bandits holding an 11-to-9 shot advantage.

The Revolution remained positive as they exited the ice for the intermission.

"Keep on working there, guys," said Coach Fitzgerald. "Let's focus on each and every shift out there. Put in the hard work, then let the next line go grind! It will be a collective effort out there. If we are pulling in the same direction, we are going to make life miserable for them."

CHAPTER XXI

GETTING TO WORK

The Kip Kelley line was set to start the second period with Freeman and Black flanking them on the backend, just like at the start of the game.

"Let's have a better start this period, boys!" announced Kip to his teammates as he circled in for another faceoff with Kirby Rollins.

Kip was the first to deliver as he cleanly won the puck away from Rollins and sent it back to his defence. Freeman cradled the puck and retreated a little as he looked for some passing lanes to emerge. He was pressured through the middle by Altoy and was forced to dish to his defensive partner. Black received the puck and immediately pushed it up the wall to where DJ had positioned himself between the redline and offensive blueline.

DJ could feel Danielsson's presence and decided to chip the puck off the wall as it came to him. Unfortunately for DJ, he still had to brace himself for a stern bodycheck from the 6'3" defender.

The chipped puck didn't quite make it beyond the goal line and that provided a solid opportunity for Kip to get in on the forecheck. Kip tracked down O'Rourke and made some contact with him in the corner as the defenceman tried to keep possession of the puck. Kip was persistent, but the captain of the Bandits was able to rim the puck hard around the boards and up the left side to his winger.

Chris Robertson managed to pick it up just inside his own blueline and direct it to Rollins as he came across the ice to support his winger. Rollins gained control and evaded an oncoming hit from Rosenberg. As Rollins stormed up and out of his zone, the shrill sound of the referee's whistle sounded and stopped his offensive attempt instantaneously.

Just across from where the Bandits' centre was breaking out of his own zone, Wallace Black and Lucas Danielsson were in the middle of a wrestling match. The big, veteran Revolution defenceman had taken exception to the hit on his underage teammate. The linesmen were able to break the two up and they were both sent to the penalty box to serve their roughing penalties. The ref motioned to both benches with his hands that play would continue on 4-on-4. JJ Turcotte and James Northgate hopped over the boards to replace the first line for the Revolution.

"All good there, DJ?" asked Kip as the two sat down next to each other on the bench.

"Yeah!" responded DJ. "All good."

"Kip and Rosenberg," announced Coach Fitzgerald from behind them. "You two back up."

Out on the ice, the team was able to create a quick turnover in the neutral zone from some good defensive work by Donald Redman. Turcotte was quick to retrieve the puck from the broken play and had his head on a swivel as he gained control. With a quick and hard flick of his wrists, he sent a perfectly-timed seam pass through the Bandits in the neutral zone and hit Northgate breaking down the right side of the ice.

Northgate took control of the puck and used his size and strength to gain an inside position on the Bandits' defender. He fought off Joel Ridley and broke in all alone on Owen Vaughn in net. Northgate took a quick glance up to see where he needed to shoot and then released the puck toward the top-right corner of the net. Vaughn was dropping into the butterfly as the big, rugged winger drew in close and the puck glanced off his shoulder on its way into the net. Northgate tied the game 1–1.

Turcotte charged into the corner after Northgate and leaped into his arms in celebration. They were joined by Redman and Sharp before skating back to their bench for a series of high-fives. On the way to the bench, everyone chanted, "Jimmy!" as they cheered on their teammate for his big goal.

Kip and Rosenberg skated back on the ice and attempted to capitalize on the newly-generated momentum, but despite hemming the Bandits in their own end for the entire duration of their shift, they came away with nothing to show for their valiant efforts. It was the same for the Revolution shift after shift, as they heavily pressed in on Owen Vaughn and the Bandits' defence for the majority of the second period. With five minutes remaining in the second, the Revolution was carrying a 16-to-3 shot advantage through the period.

When the whistle blew after Vaughn had stopped yet another shot, Coach Fitzgerald said, "All right, Turcotte. You guys go get us the lead here!"

Turcotte, Northgate and Gage's line jumped onto the ice and skated out for the offensive zone faceoff. Meeting them for the lineup was the Bandits' fourth line —Josh McCrae, Andre Iggulden and Troy Baker. The line was known for strong defensive play, but more so for being very physical. The physical intent of the line choice was evident well before the puck dropped as Baker tried to entice Northgate with some chirping and stick work as the two lined up in front of the net.

"You're the tough guy, eh!" barked Baker as he taunted Northgate. "Babysitter for that prima donna superstar, huh?"

Northgate did his best to keep his cool and stood up, looked at Baker and nodded his head. "Better believe it."

"So, you're just going to take it then, huh?" yelled Baker as he poked at Northgate in the midsection.

Once again, Northgate responded calmly, "Yeah, that's right."

The referee witnessed the events happening in front of him and skated between the two big wingers. "That's enough, boys!" the referee shouted before returning to his place in the opposite corner.

But as the puck dropped, Baker did not concur with the referee and he delivered a nasty cross-check on Northgate—right in the lower back. The blow dropped Northgate to the ice and Baker didn't hesitate to follow up his first shot with a second. Baker continued to rough up Northgate as the other Revolution players came in to support their fallen player. However, the Bandits' current line was physically dominant and manhandled their opponents as they tussled in the scrum out front of the net.

The officials were finally able to gain back control of the situation and all the players on the ice were escorted to their respective penalty boxes—minus two players. Troy Baker had received a game misconduct and was ejected from the game, while James Northgate remained on the ice. Dr. Andrews, the Revolution's trainer, made his way onto the ice with the help of Kip Kelley.

"Hey, Jimmy!" Dr. Andrews greeted the fallen player. "How's the back?"

"Bad…" replied the winger in agony.

"Anything else bothering you?" asked his trainer.

"Nah…"

"Alright. Well, take your time and we'll get you to the dressing room to check you out, okay?"

"Sounds good, Doc," responded Northgate.

The huddle lasted half a minute before Northgate was helped up to his feet and skated off to the Revolution's dressing room without any help.

The referees broke from their brief meeting and issued the penalties to the timekeeper. The Revolution would be on a 5-on-4 power play for four minutes following Baker's reckless attack on Northgate.

"Let's get one here for Jimmy, boys!" declared Coach Fitzgerald. "Kipper, take your line with Freeman and Kole on the point."

Kip and the gang skated out for the offensive zone faceoff. Lining up with Kip for the draw, once more, was Kirby Rollins.

"Can't control that monster, eh?" Kip jabbed at Rollins half seriously and half mockingly.

"Not my duty, man!" responded the skilled centre of the Bandits.

Kip laughed at the remark. "No doubt."

The two braced themselves for the puck drop, and Rollins was able to time it precisely. He won the puck back toward his defenceman. DJ was prepared to engage on a lost draw and charged in after the puck and pressured the defender. Rosenberg circled in to help his fellow wing, retrieved the puck from the battle and looped in behind the net. He was a very poised player and able to skate the puck all the way around to the hashmarks on the far wall before deciding on passing it up to Freeman at the point.

Freeman had a lane to the net to attempt a shot, but no Revolution skaters were out front, so he opted to maintain possession and instead passed it back to Rosenberg on the half wall. Kip worked his way through the slot and into the corner to give Rosenberg an option down low. Rosenberg bumped the puck down below the goal line and then skated to where he had just put the puck. Kip moved into the puck and rotated positions with Rosenberg. At the same time, DJ broke toward the front of the net and provided a screen on Owen Vaughn.

"Kipper!" shouted Kole Kelley as he streaked toward the high slot. He drew in the defenders as they attempted to take away the passing lane from an immediate shooting threat.

Kip watched patiently as the Bandits played their defensive hand, but he stayed in control of the puck. Kole circled back up to the top of the umbrella power-play formation. Kip inched out toward the blueline ever-so methodically, and then promptly sent a return pass down to Rosenberg below the goal line. Rosenberg controlled the puck and with one quick look out to the net, he sent a hard cross-crease pass to a streaking Dallas Freeman on the backdoor. Freeman connected with the one-timer and pushed the puck into the gaping cage, bringing the score to 2–1 Revolution!

"What an execution!" said an excited Kip Kelley when the players came together in the corner. "Great work!"

"Nice job, guys!" replied DJ joyfully.

"Amazing pass, Rosie!" added Freeman.

The first power-play unit had made short work of their first opportunity and stayed on the ice for the second minor penalty. The neutral zone start didn't fare well, and the

Revolution was unable to gain much traction as the clock ticked away and the second period came to a close. It had been an impressive period of action for the team as they outscored the Bandits 2–0 and outshot them 18-to-4. The two-period total in shots was 27-to-13, significantly in favour of the Revolution.

CHAPTER XXII

THIRD OVERALL ON THE LINE

Coach Fitzgerald made his way into the room before the third period of play. He quietly strutted to the middle of the room and spoke in a gentle, yet assertive tone as he addressed the team. "Alright, guys. That was a great period and we accomplished what we set out to do. But, we still have one more period to go—so don't change one bit. We need to stay hungry. We need to remain persistent. We know they will be using this break to regroup and likely change their approach, but if we keep playing a simple, fast and hard game out there, we will continue to make things difficult for them. Keep them on their heels. Make them play the full ice as they try to come back. That means be mindful of turnovers and risky plays in our end and in the neutral zone! Keep pucks deep and always—and I mean ALWAYS—have a high guy in support in the offensive zone! An expression I learned in my earlier days—twenty miles, twenty smiles! Let's go finish off the remaining 20 minutes of action and get the win, boys!'"

There was a quiet buzz stirring through the room; a group focused on the upcoming task. DJ leaned back in his seat and closed his eyes as he visualized the upcoming period. He thought about what he could do to contribute to the team's success. He also thought about how important this victory was to the team; a third-place finish in a competitive tournament would be a big deal, regardless of it only being an exhibition. It was a great opportunity for the team to establish unity and form a bond between the players that would be competing together for the rest of the season.

"Ice is ready!" announced Assistant Coach McIntosh as he popped his head inside the room.

"Let's get back at it here now," hollered Kip Kelley as he popped up from his seat. "Keep firing on all cylinders, boys!"

Everyone finished throwing on their equipment and got into line as the team headed toward the ice—including James Northgate after he had missed the remaining portion of the second period.

The third period would start at even strength as the Bandits had killed off the rest of the Troy Baker penalty before the end of the second period. Once again, the top two lines from each side were set to match up for the opening sequence. Kip moved in against Rollins and the two engaged in an aggressive battle off the opening puck drop—Rollins managed to receive some help from his wing to get the puck back to O'Rourke. The Bandits' captain took control of the puck, immediately pressed up ice and managed to reach the redline for a dump in prior to Rosenberg's ensuing bodycheck.

The Bandits' trio of Rollins, Robinson and Altoy were flying in on the attack, and Carter Riddle was forced to immediately shoot the puck high around the boards after stopping the dumped in puck behind his net.

DJ worked hard to read the play and hustled over to the wall to make a play on the rim, however, he was engaged by Lucas Danielsson as the lanky defenceman pressed in on the pinch. The two fought for possession and a quick stick from Danielsson forced the puck back down into the corner. Geoff Altoy and Wallace Black were the next two to fight over the loose puck and the forward's quick stick chipped it down below the goal line and toward his support.

Rollins skillfully scooped the puck off the wall and changed direction with a quick, tight turn as he tried to elude Kip. Rollins gave himself a split second to make a play, but he decided on continuing with possession as he skated behind the net. Kip chased Rollins and tried to keep him within a stick length, while maintaining inside position. Rollins opted to bank a pass off the boards to O'Rourke, as he knew his counterpart was playing him well defensively.

O'Rourke cradled the puck and walked the blueline. Rosenberg stayed in his shooting lane, but the Bandits' defender attempted a quick wrist shot, despite the winger's presence. The shot made its way by the first block, but Freeman provided the second line of defence and put his body in front of the puck. The puck deflected back toward the top of the circles where Kirby Rollins, once again, met the puck. Rollins didn't hesitate to fire the puck at the net and sent a low shot in on goal. Riddle repositioned himself following the blocked shot and reacted to the shot from the opposing centre—kicking the puck out.

Chris Robinson of the Bandits found himself in a gap between defenders and tracked the rebound perfectly. He swung hard at the loose puck and sent it toward the top-right corner of the net, but Riddle snared it out of the air with his glove to deny the winger the tying goal.

The whistle blew and all the Revolution skaters converged around their goaltender to salute him for his fine save. The Bandits had definitely started the period with more intensity and drive, and the Revolution were going to have to brace themselves for the attack.

The first few shifts of the period saw the Bandits return the favour from the second period, as they opened up the period with a flurry of shots and a relentless attack. The Revolution continued to use a four-line deployment, but the Bandits were rotating their top two lines out every other shift.

"Everyone needs to step up," declared Coach Fitzgerald as the play continued. "They have their top guys hitting the ice every shift. If we can hold strong and make them play defensively, we will wear them down… keep working!"

Kirby Rollins was determined to draw the game even and was dominating the play on the ice, especially when he was away from the Kip Kelley matchup. Rollins continued to press the Revolution defensively and use his linemates effectively, but Carter Riddle held his ground strongly between the pipes. Finally, after a few shifts removed from their head-to-head matchup, the Rollins and Kelley lines found themselves back on the ice together again for a faceoff to the left of Riddle.

Rollins won the draw back and Altoy jumped on the loose puck. Altoy one-touched it back to O'Rourke for a shooting opportunity, but Rosenberg rushed out forcing him to hold off and dump the puck into the corner.

Robertson moved in on the puck and received pressure from Donald Redman in the corner. Redman used his reach advantage to keep Robertson contained in the corner—which forced him to chip the puck behind the net to where Rollins just skated. Rollins controlled the puck and felt Kip on his backside. The two were circling in behind the net and Rollins made a hard play to the front of the net—resulting in Kip's stick knocking him off balance and to the ice. The puck slid free from Rollins' stick to Curtis Kraemer.

"*TWEET!*" shrilled the referee's whistle. "Tripping—number nine!" shouted the official as he pointed at Kip. The centreman couldn't believe his luck on the unfortunate play, but he made his way to the penalty box.

"Nice dive," snarled Wallace Black as he passed Rollins on his way to the corner. Rollins paid him no attention as he headed straight toward the faceoff circle to the left of Riddle.

Nick Peters joined the top line again for the power play, replacing Danielsson. Burrow, Cooke and Freeman joined Black on the penalty kill. Burrow and Rollins went in for the faceoff and the two tied up with the puck remaining between them. Cooke and Altoy barged in and tried to gain possession—their sticks poked it toward the boards where Robertson was able to take control for the Bandits. The Bandits moved the puck around the perimeter and settled into their power-play formation.

Rollins, O'Rourke and Peters moved the puck across the top of the offensive zone cleanly, while Robertson and Altoy alternated between the front of the net and their own respective corners. Rollins and Peters isolated Cooke on the one side and tried to create another scoring opportunity—much like how they had scored in the first period. Cooke played them well and had solid support as the two skilled power play forwards zipped the puck around.

Rollins gained control once again at the top of the zone and decided to change up the look. He started to skate the puck across the top and down the left wall, alternating positions with Peters. Rollins carried the puck deep into the zone.

Meanwhile behind the play, the Bandits' coach had waved his goaltender to the bench as he felt the team's pressure was suitable for the risk of leaving his net empty. Third-line centre Grahame Morrow replaced Owen Vaughn when he got to the bench.

It was now a 6-on-4 advantage for the Bandits as they pressed for the equalizer with 8:37 on the clock and 1:35 remaining in the penalty.

"Empty net!" hollered the players on the Revolution's bench.

Morrow entered the zone and drove directly to the net. Rollins saw his player streaking into the slot uncontested and delivered a perfect pass. Morrow connected with the one-timer and sent a laser through the legs of Carter Riddle—tying the game 2–2.

The Bandits celebrated and the Revolution felt deflated. Kip Kelley stepped out of the penalty box and skated toward his bench.

"Kipper… stay on," announced Coach Fitzgerald as he waved his hand toward the ice. "DJ and Trent, let's go! We are good here guys—stay cool. Let's move forward!"

The onslaught from the Bandits up to this point in the period had been a demoralizing experience for the Revolution, but the top line was prepared to battle back and give their team a chance to recapture some momentum.

The Kelley line was on the ice, but the Bandits decided that the tying goal gave them an opportunity to rest their top two lines for a shift and they utilized their third line instead. Kip won the draw from the game's latest goal scorer, Grahame Morrow.

Eric Matheson received the won faceoff and sent a D-to-D pass to Cody Ryerson—who then fed Rosenberg on the wing. The winger picked up the puck and slid it to the middle as Kip came in for support. Kip controlled it and took possession into the offensive zone.

The Bandits' defender closed Kip off and made him chip it down into the zone in order to allow DJ an opportunity at the loose puck. DJ charged into the corner and made a clean stick check on Kirk Templeton of the Bandits. This disengaged the puck and allowed DJ to take possession and curl up the boards. Kip carried on into the zone and DJ and Kip made a quick give-and-go, which allowed DJ to curl up even higher into the zone. He was given some space to step into a slapshot and fired a hard, low shot at Vaughn in net. Both Kip and Rosenberg worked hard to get to the slot and provide a screen—and a potential redirect. Kip managed to get the toe of his blade on the puck as it sizzled along the ice. The tip elevated the puck, but Vaughn challenged the shot and easily held onto it after it hit him in the chest.

"Good start, good start!" called out Kip to his line as they circled in for the next draw. "Let's build off that!"

The following faceoff was won by Kip again and the puck was slung back in behind him. Rosenberg charged in from the boards and pounded it through the oncoming block. The puck ripped toward the net and caught Owen Vaughn off guard—slightly. Vaughn instinctively dropped into the butterfly, however, at the very last second DJ lunged his stick toward the shot and was able to tip the puck. The puck redirected up and over Vaughn's shoulder—*TING!* The redirected shot nailed the crossbar and fired up and out toward the weak-side boards.

"Oh man..." DJ said to himself out loud.

Kirk Templeton was able to gather up the puck and start a breakout for the Bandits following the near-miss. The Revolution were strong through the neutral zone though, and they were able to create a turnover and dump the puck back into the offensive zone in order to make a line change.

"Way to go, guys," said Coach Fitzgerald. He came over and gave the trio a pat on the shoulders. "Perfect response!"

"Thanks, Coach!" the three said in unison.

Out on the ice, the play had noticeably evened out as the teams both tried to implement offence, while remaining strong defensively. As the final moments of the third period ticked away, the next goal was feeling more and more like it would be the game winner. Finally, the buzzer sounded and that made certain the next goal would be the deciding goal—as the game headed into sudden-death overtime.

CHAPTER XXIII

NEXT GOAL WINS

Following the guidelines of the Labour Day Classic Tournament rules, the upcoming overtime would be a ten-minute sudden-death period with play continuing on at 5-on-5; if the game were still tied it would go into a shootout.

Coach Fitzgerald huddled up the Revolution at the bench to go over some brief instruction before the game continued. "Alright here. We have given ourselves a great opportunity to achieve our goal of third place, gentlemen. We entered the tournament looking to make a statement and this is the moment we can make it—go out there and take it! Kipper, your line leads the way with Black and Freeman."

"Whoo!" sounded Kip. "Let's go get this one, boys!"

Both teams surged out to centre ice and were ready to hop into action once again. Naturally, Kirby Rollins led his team out to line up against Kip Kelley and the gang.

"Well, Rolly... next goal wins, brother!" announced Kip as the two centres faced one another.

"Indeed!" responded the skilled Bandits' centreman.

The referee motioned to each goaltender to ensure they were ready for puck drop, then as quick as a whip, he dropped the puck and the overtime began. Kip and Rollins dug in hard for the opening possession—with Rollins getting the slight advantage.

Geoff Altoy raced in ahead of DJ and was able to chip the puck back to Ryan O'Rourke. The captain received the pass and looked up ice before chipping the puck off the boards to his left winger. Robinson was there to meet the banked pass and sent it deep into the Revolution's zone.

Carter Riddle watched the puck as it was sent into the corner and came out to meet it and transition the Revolution efficiently on the breakout. Freeman and Black both raced back and positioned themselves to each side of Riddle for an easy outlet pass. Riddle was patient and drew in the oncoming check from Rollins before sending the puck behind his net to Black.

Black scooped up the puck and realized the wingers for the Bandits were taking away the outside options, so he dished to Kip as he curled in Black's direction out in the slot. The centre smoothly turned up the ice and dodged a quick stick check from Altoy as the Bandit winger pressed into the middle. Chris Robinson angled Kip as he approached the neutral zone and forced him to make a quick pass to DJ as he moved up the left wall. Instantly, Danielsson stepped up into DJ's lane, just as he had all game long. DJ was able to chip the puck by the defender and brace himself for the bodycheck—*CRASH!* Kip slid beyond the collision and gathered up the puck; Robinson remained on the chase.

"With you, Kip!" shouted Rosenberg as he came across the ice to support his linemate.

Kip heard his right winger's call and slid it to the middle. Rosenberg cradled the puck and skated over the blueline and into the Bandits' zone. Ryan O'Rourke shadowed the play and transitioned into a one-on-one with his opponent.

Rosenberg knew he didn't have much of a chance to generate more off the rush, so he opted to pull the puck back and use O'Rourke as a screen. In one motion, the puck was released through the legs of the defenceman and flying in on net—Owen Vaughn dropped into the butterfly and swallowed the puck up on the save.

The whistle sounded and the play came to a halt. The linesman rushed in and retrieved the puck from the goaltender and both teams moved in for the faceoff.

"Wasted one," said Rosenberg unhappily as he came together with Kip.

"All good, big guy," replied the centreman. "Nothing wrong with getting shots on net. Nobody else was up with you anyway. We'll get another chance!"

"Good shot, Rosie," declared DJ as he skated into the quick on-ice huddle. "Switch up off the draw?"

"Sure thing," answered Rosenberg. The two wingers switched sides, which would allow Rosenberg to come off the wall for a shot if Kip could manage a faceoff win.

Rollins, however, was the winner of the corner battle and cleanly won it back. O'Rourke gained possession and hustled to get in behind his net in order to make a breakout pass. Off the lost draw, DJ had busted through from the front of the net and applied immediate pressure on the defenceman. O'Rourke quickly realized he was in hot pursuit and rimmed the puck around the boards—allowing Dallas Freeman the opportunity to jump in and keep the play alive in the offensive zone. Freeman narrowly beat out Robinson to the boards and chipped it back into the corner.

O'Rourke carried on toward the puck and looked to the middle for support. A split-second after retrieving the puck though, he was checked by DJ who had continued in after the defender. DJ landed a strong hit and knocked his opponent off the puck—he quickly took control and headed toward the net. Rollins stopped quickly and made an effort to slow down the play, but it was just out of reach as DJ busted in on Vaughn from the corner.

DJ had his eyes set on how things were forming in front of him—Lucas Danielsson was the only defender and crouched low to take away the passing lane to Kip out front of the net, and Vaughn was playing any shooting play aggressively. DJ was running out of time to make a decision as he closed in. He looked to Kip but sent a quick shot high on net—the puck sailed through the air and over Vaughn's shoulder as he dropped down into the signature butterfly. The puck rang off the crossbar and deflected down into the goal; DJ had scored the overtime winning goal!

DJ jumped in the air as he witnessed the puck enter the net and was instantaneously mobbed by his teammates on the ice—the players from the bench jumped the boards and flooded the ice to join the celebration!

"Way to go, DJ!" howled Kip while they were confined together in the middle of the players. "Going to have to start calling you 'Mr. Clutch'!" he laughed joyfully.

"Thanks, Kip!" replied DJ with a smile.

DJ was overjoyed and completely captivated by the moment. He received praise from his teammates for his remarkable work and wonderful game-winning goal. As the celebration began to dwindle, he glanced up into the stands. There standing and celebrating, were his parents, as well as Marty and his parents. The blissful event immediately subsided from his mind, and he began to think about Marty heavily. He watched as his best friend showed complete admiration for what the team had just accomplished—all the while knowing his own fate was still up in the air.

"Hey, Kip!" shouted DJ as the players started to skate away.

Kip turned around with a smile plastered on his face. "What's up, hero?"

"I… I just want to say," DJ began nervously, "you have been a great leader and supporter for me throughout the camp…"

"Hey, man… you deserve it!"

"I ahh… I was really upset and angry with you after your hit on Marty. I just want to let you know that any issues I had pent up inside of me are gone. Umm…"

"I get it, DJ. He's your best bud! I maybe took things a bit far… and looked for a chance to hit him. I feel bad to have put him out," Kip said remorsefully. "You don't have to say anything to me—I understand what you both must be going through…"

"Yeah… I do need to get it out, though," sighed DJ. "If only for my own peace of mind. You have been very important to my success throughout the camp. I just want our relationship to remain strong, and not have anything left unresolved."

"Thanks, man… and I truly am sorry!" Kip extended his hand and the two players clasped their hands together and gave each other a hug.

CHAPTER XXIV

THE AFTERMATH

The players and coaching staff from both teams lined up for ceremonial handshakes following the Revolution's victory—DJ was congratulated by his opposition for his valiant effort on the game-winning goal. As the teams finished cycling through, they both left the ice and returned to their respective dressing rooms. Coach Fitzgerald and his assistants followed their players into the room.

"Very well done!" Coach Fitzgerald began. "I am very proud of the effort each and every one of you displayed—not just in this game—but the entire tournament! We had a young lineup in Game #1, against a very strong team, and took a loss. However, we came here to learn what we can expect from all of our players; we gave everyone an opportunity to show their ability. Games #2 and #3 were great showings and I think it is fair to say we exceeded "outsider" expectations here this weekend. So, congratulations to all of you!"

Coach Fitzgerald stopped and retrieved his clipboard from Assistant Coach Horton. "Having said that, we do have some final decisions to make as we look to go forward and enter the start of the season. For those of you that remain unsigned, we will need to meet with you to discuss our plans with you. For the rest of you, we will be meeting up for office conditioning Tuesday evening. Good day, gentlemen!"

The coaching staff exited the dressing room and moved along to meet up with management in order to finalize their roster.

"Good game, Coach!" beamed GM Bob Flaherty as the he stood up to shake the hand of his head coach when they arrived in the stands.

"Thanks, Bob," replied Coach Fitzgerald. The coaching staff moved in and situated themselves accordingly. "Decision time!"

"Decision time…" responded the group in unison.

"If I could offer my outlook first, that would be appreciated," said GM Flaherty rhetorically. "I was very impressed with the play of our young guys out there. Underagers, specifically, all played very well and have made a strong case for themselves. But when I put my pen to my paper and create a lineup, it never changes my decision on who my remaining underage card will be used on: Marty. I understand Marty's situation, but I could live without regret passing on the other guys—even though I appreciate their talents. I couldn't say the same thing if Martinsen was let go."

"Injury aside," began Assistant Coach Horton, "he was the best player in the mini-camp, in my opinion."

"I get it," responded Coach Fitzgerald. "I honestly do. But I am reserved on what an injury of this nature could present going forward. What timeline is he going to be on? That is uncertain. What further complications could there be? Unknown."

"That's exactly it," agreed Assistant Coach McIntosh. "What if he can't play or doesn't play up to form following this injury? Letting a young D or a Burrow go free—potentially being picked up by another team—when they could be a key component to our team."

"Break down our lineup without them then," insisted GM Flaherty. "Are we strong enough at each position? I think we are. Which to me states that if you have the best player available to choose, you take the best player regardless of the complications he may or may not endure in his recovery! Assume that he is more than capable of returning to form and that he will be a huge addition to the projected lineup when he is back and ready to go."

"Okay, Bob," announced Coach Fitzgerald. "Let's formulate a mock lineup without a second underage card then."

The group worked together to come up with a formidable lineup that they could agree on:

Forwards:
DJ Roberts – Kip Kelley – Trent Rosenberg
Harrison Gage – JJ Turcotte – Jeremy Wright
Dominic O'Connor – Kole Kelley – James Northgate
Anson Brown – Stewart Cooke – Joel Stevenson

Defence:
Wallace Black – Dallas Freeman
Curtis Kraemer – Donald Redman
Andrew Boersman – Cody Ryerson

Goaltenders:
Carter Riddle
Spencer McIntyre

Forward Scratches: Steve Reinhart and Scott Parker
Defensive Scratch: Martin Killington

"So, that gives us 14 forwards, 7 defencemen and 2 goalies before making a decision on the second underage card," proclaimed GM Flaherty.

The group discussed the matter for a while longer as they awaited the arrival of the first player to visit with them. They worked feverishly and ultimately came to a conclusion.

"So, we are all good with this decision, gentlemen?" asked GM Flaherty. He held up the sheet of paper he was jotting the lineup and notes on.

"We are good!" they stated together.

DING!

The sound of DJ's cell phone alerted him to an incoming text message and the young hockey player reached out to pick up his phone.

"Great job tonight, buddy!" read Marty's message.

DJ smiled as he read the compliment from his best friend. He finished getting changed and then started typing a response. *"Thanks man! Nice way to finish heading into the season!"*

"No doubt. GM Flaherty sent me a text—have a meeting with the coaching staff and management tomorrow morning…" he replied quickly.

DJ took a moment to digest what he just read. He immediately wondered what the plan would be for Marty.

"Hoping for the best!" Marty added before DJ had a chance to write something back.

"Yes! Same here!" he wrote back quickly. And then he began a new message. *"I am sure that whatever happens is for the best pal… you showed what you are capable of before getting*

hurt... no denying that! I am positive you will be right beside me when you are ready to go!"

"*Thanks... appreciate that DJ!"* responded Marty. *"I will meet up with you after the meeting if that is cool??"*

"*Sure thing! See you tomorrow!"* replied DJ. DJ picked up his gear and said goodbye to the remaining players in the room. He gathered up his sticks and then left. He couldn't stop thinking about Marty's situation following their brief conversation. What would the outcome be? He couldn't imagine going through this journey without his best friend—they were inseparable. As much fun as he was having thus far, he knew that things would be that much greater if they could share the experience together. But how serious was this injury? And how could that influence the Revolution's decision making?

CHAPTER XXV

THE FINAL CUT

It was officially Labour Day and the last day of summer break before high school commenced—DJ was using it as a recuperation day from the exhausting and gruelling weekend. Having played a prominent role in all three games and as the focus of the opposition's defensive plan, he had taken a lot of abuse physically during the tournament. His very sore body reminded him of the punishment he had endured. As he rolled out of bed, the sharp pain in his ribs reminded him of the combination of cross-checks and bodychecks he had suffered. He managed to push through the agony and get to his feet.

DJ went downstairs and sought out the local newspaper so he could read the scoop from the weekend. He found it in the living room and flipped through to the sports section. Headlining the section was Dean Moore's recap of the Labour Day Classic Tournament.

Revolution Earn Third Place
by Dean Moore

A three-game prep tournament came to a close yesterday with our hometown Junior A Revolution earning third overall after an exciting 3–2 overtime win over the Bandits. DJ Roberts was the eventual overtime hero as he converted on a solo effort to clinch the victory.

The Bandits came out early and opened up the scoring on a power-play goal from Nick Peters. They were able to hold onto their lead throughout the first period, but the Revolution stormed back in the second period and completely dominated the play. They outscored the Bandits 2–0 and outshot them significantly with goals coming from James Northgate and Dallas Freeman. Earning assists for the Revolution were JJ Turcotte, Trent Rosenberg and Kip Kelley. The Bandits came back revitalized in the third period though, and scored another power-play goal—off the stick of Grahame Morrow this time—to tie the game and send it into extra-time. Roberts then secured the win just 33 seconds into overtime after stripping the puck away from the Bandits' captain, Ryan O'Rourke, in the corner and walking out to beat goaltender Owen Vaughn with a high, short-side wrister.

While the victory was an important team-builder, the tournament's primary objective was to evaluate and determine the team's roster as it heads into opening night next Friday. "We sure were happy with the win," Coach Fitzgerald said, "but more importantly, we were able to find out what we can expect from certain players and figure out where all the puzzle pieces fit."

General Manager Bob Flaherty was unable to release the final roster for the team before the time of publication, but noted it would be available prior to their Tuesday night's off-ice training session. "We have our team selected and all players that have been released following the tournament have been offered affiliation cards. Whether they choose to venture elsewhere, that is their decision. But we wished them all success with their upcoming year and hope to see them back next year."

Following the Revolution's win, a clash of the league's semi-final matchup last season commenced in the finals—as the Hawks squared up with the Jaguars. Last season in the playoffs, the Jaguars were able to oust the Hawks in seven games. However, the refurbished Hawks were able to garner up some redemption to kick off the new season as they captured a 2–1 overtime win to claim the Labour Day Classic championship!

DJ had stayed to watch the championship game and do some scouting of his competition for the year. He witnessed a high-paced game with a lot of intensity—especially for a pre-season matchup. However, he was well aware of the playoff rivalry the two had last year and knew that both teams had many players returning to their respective teams this season.

Last year, after eliminating the Hawks in Game #7, the Jaguars had moved on to face a relatively fresh Panthers hockey club, who had polished off their first two rounds in convincing fashion and sported an 8–1 record heading into the regional final. The Jags gave the Panthers all they could handle, but ultimately lost in a hard-fought seven-game series. Fortunately for the Jaguars, they were set to host the Central Championship and had moved on to the round robin tournament regardless—with the winner to advance to the National Championship. The Jaguars didn't fare so well, but the Panthers had advanced to the finals where they eventually lost to the Terriers 3–1, despite opening up the tournament with a win over them and going undefeated in the round robin matchups.

Setting down the newspaper, DJ grabbed the remote control to turn on the television and tuned into the sports channel to watch the morning highlights. While hockey was his main love, DJ was very active in numerous sports and always enjoyed watching—with soccer and baseball being his favourite secondary options.

DING! DJ glanced at his phone.

"Meeting's all done—you just at home?" read Marty's text.

"Sure am, boss! Slide on by anytime…" replied DJ.

"Sounds good! I will be by in about 15 minutes."

"Any spoilers on how things went before you get here???"

Marty didn't get back to him with a response, so DJ placed his phone down and continued to watch the TV as he rested in wait for his friend's arrival.

KNOCK! KNOCK! KNOCK!

The sound of the door jolted him up from the recliner like a cannon going off. DJ rushed toward the door and opened it up.

"Quick service!" Marty joked as the two exchanged a fist bump.

"Only the best service here, my friend!" laughed DJ. "C'mon in!"

The two walked into the living room and sat down. DJ grabbed the remote and put the show on mute. "Well," DJ began excitedly, "you're not going to keep me hanging here are you? How did the meeting go?"

"It was pretty interesting," Marty replied. "All the management and coaching staff were there and so was Dr. Andrews."

"Oh?"

"Yeah, they went over a lot of things regarding my injury—or injuries for that matter. They are concerned that I may be unable to return to action and whether I would be able to compete at this level if I were to come back. Understandable, I guess…" Marty explained.

"Yeah, I guess so," responded DJ, unnerved.

"Dr. Andrews said he has seen different responses to whiplash and concussion injuries," Marty continued on. "Said it could be as quick as one week, but it is always an indefinite experience depending on the individual and severity of the trauma."

"Do they think you are in bad shape? Or are they just taking precaution in regards to the situation?" DJ questioned.

"Bit of both… maybe," Marty pondered.

DJ thought for a moment. "Well, that's disheartening—I thought this was going to be a different conversation."

"I wish it were," replied Marty sadly.

"Hmm…" DJ sighed. He wasn't even sure how to console his best friend at this moment while the two sat in silence, glancing up at the television.

"But…" Marty interjected, breaking the silence, "I do have some good news to share!"

DJ looked surprised. "Okay?"

"They have decided they are willing to take a risk with my health… and they offered me the second underage card!" Marty said with a smile.

DJ was astonished by the way Marty had played with his emotions. "Are you kidding me?" he said excitedly.

"Dead serious," Marty laughed as if he was enjoying toying with his friend's feelings.

"So, you signed?" DJ asked.

"Even have the ink mark on my pinky finger to show for it," Marty said and he held up his hand to show the ink blot left behind from his hand streaking across the freshly signed card.

DJ stood up. "You little stinker!" he laughed as he went over to properly congratulate Marty with a handshake.

"You know what this means, right?" Marty asked as he grasped DJ's hand. "We get to write a whole new story together, once again!"

Manufactured by Amazon.ca
Bolton, ON